ALFRED'S TANGO
and
Other Unlikely
Tales

ALFRED'S TANGO
and Other Unlikely Tales

Chris Curtis

Alfred's Tango

First published 2019

Copyright © 2018 Chris Curtis

Published by Palm Garden Publishers
Email: palmgardenpress@optusnet.com.au

Set in 10/12 pt Garamond

Cover by Palm Garden Publishers

National Library of Australia
Cataloguing-in-Publication data:
Author: Chris Curtis
Title: Alfred's Tango and Other Unlikely Tales
ISBN-13: 978-0-9872580-1-4

***

Dedication

The stories in this book were first read by my wife and muse, June Curtis without whose gentle criticism and insight I would be voiceless. Thank you June, for many years of love, support and inspiration.

My mother Frances Curtis deserves her own book. She raised her family in the face of tragedy with stoicism, hard work and endurance. She never managed to teach me to spell, but her intelligence, high principles and infinite mind took me to places of wonder and fascination. Part of her is in this book.

My brother Tony died before he could start a book and our son, Jeffrey before he had the chance; both of you are here.

To our daughter Kathryn and Jeremy, James and Sara Martens, I hope that you enjoy these stories and remember that everything is possible.

Contents

Lost and Found

Dark clouds raced from behind, streaming northward across the harbour, the water mirroring the sky in angry turmoil, streaks of foam defining the sandstone sea walls. In the distance office buildings and rooftops seemed to fade into the murky background as Grogan looked down from the high window.

He couldn't feel the wind but he knew what to expect.

Looks like we're in for a storm, he thought.

He turned abruptly. 'I'm not sure exactly what we can do, Ron. A garbled piece of intelligence! A vague clue! It's not much to go on.'

'Yes, I know, but ASIO can only give us what they can winkle out of the Americans. And that's all we've got.'

'What *have* we got?' asked Grogan, counting on his fingers.

'One: *reliable* information there'll be an attack on Sydney in the next few days; and two: the attack will be coordinated with clandestine messages placed in the "Lost and Found" section of *The Herald* - messages possibly mentioning a bird of some kind.' His voice expressed amusement and annoyance. 'It sounds like something from a Raymond Chandler novel. We don't even know the name of the group!'

'Yes, I know,' said the other man in a resigned tone. 'You'll just have to do the best you can. I know you will.'

Grogan knew he was getting everything there was to give. They'd known each other for a long time; first in the field, and then when working in different directions through the bureaucracy.

It was up to him to put it together.

'Ok,' he sighed, 'I'll see what I can find out.'

They parted with the usual formalities.

Outside, violent thunder struck the city; yet Grogan heard none of it as he descended to his own office.

Across the city, oblivious to the coming storm, Brenda Watson watched the morning kettle boil. The sound of bubbling surged to a climax as she waited patiently for the whistle: a lonely noise telling her to do something, to take action. And that was good! *One day she'd get an electric jug, though not just yet.*

Water steamed as she poured it into the old china teapot and fitted the chipped lid. She spun the teapot twice and dressed it in a black and yellow tea cozy. Breakfast tea was a comforting ritual, and now mother had gone, she could not think of any reason to stop.

Rituals, habits; these things kept her going.

The funeral had been a trial; and then the constant appearance of her mother's friends at the house, an annoyance. *Nice people, but she wanted to meet new faces.*

Her own friends had moved away long ago.

She wanted to meet other people; perhaps she would look for a job. It had been so long.

She left the tea to draw and walked down the hall, her slippers making dull flapping noises on the carpet, instinctively checking her appearance in the hall mirror as she passed.

A little overweight yet still slim, her brown hair now greying, she'd once been considered good looking.

She adjusted an errant strand of hair and turning to the front door, opened it and walked to the front gate. *Might do a spot of gardening later,* she mused as she checked for the mail and newspaper; *but then again, maybe not* as she heard the distant thunder, noted the dark clouds, gathered the contents of the box, and returned to the house.

Back in the kitchen, she looked at the mail and threw both envelopes into the waste paper bin, then opened the cut-glass doors of the cabinet and reached for the antique cup and saucer standing alone on the shelf.

The chair scraped as she pulled it out and sat down. Brenda relished using the delicate porcelain cup and matching saucer. Her mother would never permit it.

"It's too precious, Brenda, you might break it." *It's more precious now you've gone,* she thought.

She turned her attention to the paper.

The reportage of widespread murder and violence did not interest her much.

She turned to the crossword - another ritual.

7 down: Fond of company, sociable (10).

Gregarious she said as she filled in the letters.

Yes, that describes me perfectly, the bitter irony of her words causing her to take stock of her thoughts. *I really must do something. Make some changes. Get a life!*

She looked into space for a long moment.

But what can I do?

3

She did not work, had no social life, almost no friends and, apart from the funeral and essential shopping, she'd not been out of the house for months.

After another long pause and a sip of tea, she returned to the newspaper. Near the business section, she noticed the *Lost and Found* column. Most days it only contained plaintive appeals for lost dogs and cats!

Though *sometimes*, something interesting appeared!

"You can tell people's lives from what they lose," her mother had always said.

In his office, Grogan slumped in his chair and sipped his coffee. He was never comfortable sitting down; too big, and now a tad overweight, despite his rigorous exercise regime

His discomfort didn't improve his mood.

In his years in the Federal Police, he'd developed an instinct and knew the chances of a successful conclusion to this new case were very slim. There was so little to go on and the only strategy was to prepare and wait for the enemy to make the first move.

He'd alerted the local police, of course. He pitied them; *yet what could they do?*

The chair groaned as he reached for his telephone and called in his assistant. 'Jenny, the Lost and Found Case; I want you to keep your eye on all the Sydney papers. The warning only mentioned *The Herald*, but we don't want to take any chances. Include the local rags. You'll have to contact the papers directly. I want to know about this ad before the paper hits the street. Then contact Bill Wright and have him prepare the paperwork for telephone surveillance on a mobile phone ... no, two phones: a mobile and a home phone. We've only got a few days, so we'll have to be quick if something turns up.'

Alone again, he looked at the closing door for a second then picked up a file. The chances of success were depressing; the cost of failure unimaginable. Everything on the line, he wondered what more could he do now.

He hated the waiting, fearing all the time he'd missed something important.

Outside, torrents of rain fell on the city.

Grogan opened the file.

In her kitchen, Brenda glanced out the window and shook her head. Wind whipped the trees and whistled in the window cracks. Splatters of rain struck the glass. *Blast, there goes the gardening.*

She returned to the paper and glanced down the page. The first few entries were indeed about lost moggies and much-loved canines. I thought animals had homing instincts, she mused. Then she read:

Lost. Pet cockatiel.
Sometimes answers to the name of "Birdy."
Last seen in Willoughby, Saturday 25th; about 6pm.

She skimmed across the numbers of a mobile telephone. *Poor thing, it's probably dead already in this weather.*

She remembered her own childhood pet, now long gone. Perhaps this bird was also a child's pet, and the family in mourning; losing a pet is akin to losing a member of the family.

A sudden flash of inspiration!

Why speculate?

I could meet this family from Willoughby.

I just need to ring and claim to have found the bird!

She could always claim she'd made a mistake if things became difficult: a simple error; a coincidence; wrong colour; a second escape from a cage! Plenty of possibilities!

She reached hurriedly for the phone.

Any delay and she might change her mind.

She entered the number and listened to the ringing tone.

'Hello' (a man, slight accent, his voice low and questioning).

'Hello, did you advertise in *The Herald* for a lost cockatiel?'

'Err …, yes I did. Have you found it?'

'I don't know. It could be a budgerigar. I found it on Monday afternoon; in Chatswood, actually. It has a lot of white on it. Does yours have any special marks or anything?'

'Ah … I …. Are you alone at the moment?'

'Alone? Yes, but what has that to do with anything?'

'Well, you just gave me the … No, it's just that … It's nothing, can I ring you back?'

'Err… yes, of course,' said Brenda.

Such a strange person! thought Brenda after she'd divulged eight digits and hung up the phone.

It's almost as if he didn't want the bird back.

The telephone rang.

She recognised the male voice. 'I will come tomorrow to look at the bird. My name is Manak. Where do you live?' he said without preamble.

'Mm … I don't know. Could I come to your place?' *Rudeness!*

'I've got something important on at the moment. Should be over in a few days, and would be better if I called on you before then. I'll be on the road anyway.'

'Well …. OK. I live at 13 Daggers Close.'

'I'll be there at 11:00 tomorrow.'

'Yes alright, thanks very much.'

She put down the phone, looked at it thoughtfully for a few minutes, and then picked up the newspaper again.

Rain drummed on the roof.

The morning was almost past.

Later that day Inspector Grogan took a long telephone call. He answered it curtly and listened. The other person had a great deal to say. Grogan just scribbled occasionally in a small notebook and grunted from time to time. Finally, he finished the call and pressed the intercom button. 'Get the squad ready, Jenny,' he said energetically, 'things are finally moving. We need to talk to a few people.'

He snatched his coat from the back of the chair and had one arm in it as he left the office.

He noticed the sky was clearing. Patches of sunlight appeared through thin dusk clouds.

It will be a busy night but at least it would be dry.

After a sleepless night, Brenda woke late feeling seedy and listless. The storm having blown itself out, the morning was bright and sunny. The yoghurt and sliced fruit breakfast did not revive her very much.

She'd thought about yesterday's phone conversation, tossing and turning much of the night, deciding she'd been very silly, stupid really.

She decided the joke had gone far enough. A moment of grief and loneliness and she'd done a silly thing. She would ring this Manak person back and tell him someone else had claimed the bird. Or that it had died; or some other story!

She crossed the kitchen, picked up the phone and entered the number.

Nobody answered.

Eventually, a recorded voice came on the line and, in turn, she explained the situation in a message: *It was a budgerigar, and the wrong colours anyway.*

Trusting Manak to check his messages, she hung up with a sigh of relief, glad to be rid of the problem. There was something very odd about the matter. *That Manak sounded like a strange, cold person*; and the whole situation seemed quite wrong.

An hour later, a butcherbird was calling as Brenda came in from the garden and sat down for her usual cup of tea. She noted the bird absently and relished its pleasant call. She felt particularly good; the events of the last day an epiphany. She'd crossed some kind of barrier, she decided, reached a point where the past would not be regretted and she could now think about her future and push on to a new life.

She would go to Chatswood, have her hair done and buy a new electric jug.

She might even take in a movie.

As for the day after, well … it was up to her to make her future.

She'd find someone.

She'd never be lonely again.

She heard the front gate clatter and pattered to the door. A strange man was walking up the path. *Manak, of course, but what was he doing here? Why didn't he park in the driveway? Had the message not got through?*

She studied him curiously from behind the curtains. Of average height, with thinning brown hair and broad shoulders he appeared to lean forward, advancing with a narrow face and a fixed smile of perfect white teeth. *Like a shark,* thought Brenda.

His light grey business suit accentuated the appearance.

She opened the front door and waited as he approached.

He smiled broadly.

'You must be Manak.'

'Yes,' he said; and kept walking; stepping through the door as though she'd already invited him in, forcing Brenda backwards towards the kitchen in surprise.

'Nice place you have here, Brenda,' he said as he surveyed the hall.

Regaining her poise Brenda noticed more details - scuffed shoes and a stained tie - and decided she did not like Mr. Manak and his arrogant and over-familiar ways.

She would need to get this over with, as quickly as possible. 'What are you doing here? I left a message on your phone. I don't have your bird.'

His face took on a wild predatory look as lips thinned and the shark smile stretched into a snake-like smirk. 'Yes, I know. I got your message. But you gave all the right answers to our code. I need to know how much you know. What you want.'

He closed the door behind him, cutting her off from the outside world.

Brenda felt her panic rising.

'What answers? I don't know what you're talking about. I think you'd better leave. I don't have your bird,' her voice sounding shrill as she tried to edge him towards the door.

He did not move. 'Yes, that's the strange thing. Bird's lost; bird's found. And you knew the code.'

'I tell you, I don't know anything about any damned code. Why would there be a code? I'd like you to go now, please,' her anger rising.

'You know, Brenda, I don't believe in chance. Is this some sort of scam? Do you want money?'

'For the last time, I don't know what you're talking about. Please go, or I'll call the police.'

'Yes, that occurred to me, too. You know about the bird. And you now know what I look like. You thought you'd make some money somehow; and I think you've learned things. You know too much. I'm here to fix that.'

He advanced on her slowly, his teeth parted, forcing her to retreat into the kitchen. She backed against the stove, and opened her mouth to scream. Too late, his huge hand gagged her mouth. She struggled to tear it away, but he was too strong for her.

He reached behind her and selected a knife from the neatly arranged block on the shelf.

She raised her hands, fluttering them at him uselessly, trying to ward him off.

He pushed her head further back, exposing her throat as his knife hand prepared for the final slash.

The house exploded with sudden sound!

Crashes! Shouts!

And sharp commands!

Manak froze for a moment in shocked surprise, then his eyes widened and his back arched. Before he could react another hand appeared and grasped his knife hand. 'I'll take that,' said a large man.

Caught by surprise Manak tried to turn and fight off the unknown attacker, squealing and lashing backwards with his head and feet until his other hand was caught in a vice-like grip, the hold increasing painfully until he dropped the knife.

Brenda managed to wriggle away from the stove, and watched in astonishment as her attacker was spun and smashed against the wall.

An ornament fell.

Manak continued to struggle, even as his arm was twisted behind his back. Slowly his struggles subsided as handcuffs were produced and applied.

Men in dark uniforms and helmets appeared and dragged him away head bowed and sobbing.

A young female in another uniform positioned herself at Brenda's elbow. 'I'm sure it's all been a bit of a shock. Here, sit down and I'll make a cup of tea before we do anything else.'

Brenda let herself be seated and sat numbly as the girl lit the gas and put the kettle on to boil. 'It's lucky we got here in time. At least we had your address.' Brenda knew she was chatting; giving her time to recover, and was grateful as she was too confused to make conversation.

More voices and the sound of boots on floorboards issued from the back of the house until these subsided and the large man appeared at the door almost blocking it with his presence.

He pulled out a chair and sat down at the kitchen table. His brown eyes studied Brenda carefully. 'Sorry about your front door, Mrs. Watson. My name is Grogan, Inspector Grogan. I'm with the Federal Police. My officer could see what was happening through the window and thought we should act as quickly as possible.'

Is this an attempt at humour?

'It's Miss Watson, actually. How ... how did you know?' She tried to comb her hair with her fingers.

'Oh, it was no problem, really,' said Grogan lightly. 'Your phone call flushed them out. They didn't know who you were so they telephoned each other.' He shook his head, 'We were confused at first too, but eventually realised you were genuine; an innocent bystander, as it were.'

He spoke reassuringly. 'I can't tell you much, but you don't know what a great service you've done. You've saved a lot of lives, Brenda.' Her eyes widened in astonishment. 'I'll need you to come into our office if you can, and make a full statement.' He smiled pleasantly - *he's quite good looking, actually* - 'There will need to be an official investigation, but I'm sure you won't be involved.

'However, there's only one thing that puzzles me.'

He regarded her with a concerned frown.

'We've searched the whole house, but where is the bird?'

Waiting

Julia heard the phone and put down her brush. *Too early for Alice?* She descended a couple of steps and set the ladder rocking as she snatched a rag from a strut. *The ceiling will have to wait!*

The boys could not have reached the creek yet.

Perhaps there was trouble.

Maybe Alex had come off his motorbike?

The others were experienced but her youngest still thought of himself as indestructible.

Maybe they'd found that old scrub bull a little hard to handle?

Running now from the other end of the house she reached the hall and plucked the receiver from its cradle. 'Hello ...?'

'Oh, hello Julia, it's Bruce Latter. Nothing to worry about! I just thought I'd ring around and let people know about that bloke ...'

'Oh, g'day Bruce, you're ringing awfully early! Has something happened?'

'No, just doing a policeman's duty. That bloke, Weadal, is still in the area and I'm just advising everyone to take sensible precautions. Lock up your guns and ammo; don't leave tools or food lying around; don't open your door to strangers; that sort of thing. You know what I mean.'

'Yeah, sure, though we won't feel safe until you blokes catch him. When will that be?'

'We'll get him Julia, don't worry. We're getting reinforcements from the city. We'll catch him soon.'

'Bull, Bruce! Those city blokes'll be useless. They'll be too busy tip-toeing around cow pats and swatting flies.'

'Yeah, well ...'

Julia put down the phone and restarted painting the ceiling. It wasn't Bruce Latter's fault. She should've been easier on him. He was only trying to help. Still, this man had been on the run for a long time in the mountains along the border. They should've caught him, and now he'd moved south. Alice said he'd already killed several people and knew the bush well.

Alice called at ten.

As she ran to the phone again, Julia realised how much she enjoyed their chats. Alice wasn't the sharpest chisel in the set, but she was a good and reliable friend.

Julia told her about Bruce Latter's call. Alice thought the police were not telling half of what Weadal had done, to prevent panic.

Yet she was more interested in fresh news.

'Bill Johnson's hurt himself badly; and is not likely to survive. Beryl went looking when he didn't come home for lunch. She found him under his tractor about a mile from the house. Couldn't do much for him! She tried the neighbours at Booraroo, and eventually Harry Larson's boys came over and got him into town. Beryl's pretty upset. I'll drop around this afternoon.' *Bush life as usual then.*

Twenty minutes later Julia felt she'd caught up with the news. She interrupted Alice, replaced the receiver and returned to the bedroom and the fast-drying brushes.

She'd painted another arm's reach of cornice before she realised her mind was not on the job. She put down the brush again, sighed and packed away the paint. She enjoyed painting, it was relaxing and the concentration excluded all other thoughts. Though the chance to relax had passed, and there were things to be done.

Moving quickly she left the house and crossed the gravel drive. Winter clouds conquered the morning sun and cast the outbuildings and cattle yards in gloomy shadow. Entering the garage she started the town car and moved it to the front of the house. *Pity they didn't have another dog.* She would talk to Alan. The barn doors were heavy, sagging on their hinges. She finally pulled them closed and fixed the lock. The garage doors followed in turn before she returned to the house, satisfied.

Most windows latched without difficulty. The old casement window in the lounge was jammed with generations of old paint and refused to move. She left it. If she couldn't move it Weadal probably couldn't either.

She smiled; occupied, possibly with visitors; that is how it must look. It would not deter a desperate man. She gambled: *someone who could beat a woman to death would not be courageous.*

She couldn't remember if the doors to the house had ever been bolted in the years the family had lived there. Now she was grateful someone had provided for the possibility. Doors locked she moved to the kitchen.

Light rain sprinkled the window as she checked the latch.

She turned on the light over the stove.

With little thought, she chopped vegetables and pulled a leg of lamb from the freezer. She'd lost count of the lamb roasts she'd prepared. She made herself a salad. *No word from Alan and the boys*, but she didn't expect them to return while there was light, despite the weather. And she would not contact them. *They probably had their hands full with the scrubbers by now.*

She took a cup of tea into the hall and opened the gun cupboard. A few minutes work and she'd moved all the ammunition - except for one 12 gauge cartridge - to the office where it now hid as an incongruous accessory behind the A4 paper. She then lifted the shotgun from its rack, loaded the cartridge and closed and locked the cupboard door. *If he got into the house he would get the .22 but it was not much use without ammunition!*

The afternoon light was fading as she returned to the kitchen. The midday sounds of crows and the rustling of leaves had already ceased. Only the creaking and straining of the old building disturbed the silence.

She turned on the radio, music filled the room. She turned it off again. She needed to hear, to listen through the darkness.

She made another cup of tea and settled in the kitchen with the *Herald*, and the gun.

A clatter of boots.

Voices on the veranda. Muffled curses and loud thumping.

'Who locked this bloody door?'

Smoothing her apron, Julia uncocked the gun, and placed it in the corner as she slid the latch.

'Hello darling; back so soon; how did it go?' forcing a smile.

'A bull and two heifers! That'll have to do for a while! What've you been up to?' Alan was already in his socks as he stepped into the kitchen.

'Oh, just a bit of painting; and I thought the boys would enjoy a roast for dinner.'

'You should be more careful, Julia, the place is lit up like a Christmas tree.'

'Yes, dear,' she said as she kissed him on the lips.

Restoration

We met in the *Hero of Waterloo*. The bar was packed with the usual lunchtime crowd of workers from city building sites and journalists from the press offices around the corner. I looked among them for the short stocky fellow I remembered from years before. A stranger's eye met mine in the mirror backing the bar and he turned to me with a warm greeting.

'Graham, I hardly recognised you. You've put on weight.'

'Yeah, you were a bit hard to spot too, with your face-fungus,' I replied, gripping his hand.

He stroked his salt-and-pepper beard fondly.

'I've had it so long, I'd forgotten,' he said.

As we talked my mind slowly updated its mental image of him until the rotund figure in the khaki shirt and scuffed Blundstone boots became Steve again.

'You've lost a bit of hair, too,' he observed smiling.

'That why I made it a number two,' I laughed. 'I don't like a comb-over. And I can cut it myself.

The preliminaries over we were quiet for a moment until he broke the silence.

What are you up to these days?'

'Oh, pretty much the same. General chippy work most of the time. Occasionally I get some restoration work like we used to. What about you?'

'Mm, it's pretty good. It was hard going until I built up a reputation, now it's OK.'

He mentioned a firm of builders specialising in restoration work. I recognised the name. 'Yeah, that's me; I've got my boys in with me so it's a family affair now.'

We took our beers to a small table overlooking the almost empty beer garden. Steve sat on a stool and waited while I took two coasters from a small pile and placed his brimming glass on the small square of paper. For a long moment the only sound came from a badly adjusted air conditioning unit that tried - with limited success - to reduce the oppressive heat.

I continued the ritual, telling him about my work on the town hall and how difficult it was. He countered with his current work on an old staircase at the Masonic Hall.

'Can't find any seasoned cedar any more. I got some from a demolition site in the city; not much. Funny isn't it, how you've got to demolish something old and beautiful to restore something old and beautiful?' He spoke in his slow laconic way, and I had to agree with him though I'd not remembered a philosophic bent in the old Steve.

A shadow seemed to pass across the sun turning the beer garden into a gloomy forest. The sounds of the drinkers behind me matched the muffled throb of the distant traffic. I heard myself say, 'This Masonic Hall, does it have any ghosts?'

'None I've noticed! Just a lot of pigeons and a few rats!'

He must've noticed how I didn't smile at his exaggerated humour; how I stopped listening and looked into my glass, a memory pouring into my mind like a dam bursting.

I shivered.

It was a few seconds before I heard him say, 'Are you OK?'

I pulled myself together and told him the story. 'It was very strange. I'd been doing some work on the old rectory at St. Matthew's, the old convict-built church in Windsor; all brick, except for the foundations, with a slate roof, bell tower, that sort of thing. The rectory's the same, though more like an old house overhung with old camphor laurels. It was pretty run down then and hadn't been occupied for years. Someone had given my name to Mr. Reynolds, the Verger.'

I waited while Steve went to the bar for another couple of beers.

'Mr. Reynolds asked me to patch up some of the plasterwork around the windows and skirting. Naturally, I felt honored to do even a minor task on such a famous old building. It was just a small job, so I decided to fit it in after my usual work and agreed to meet him at the church the following day.

That night I slept badly for some reason and I felt a bit hung over when I arrived at the church.

I parked my van in Greenway Crescent and walked across the cemetery, skirting the overhanging trees. As I approached the church, I imagined it covered in crude scaffolding, convicts working in the open sun, an overseer lounging under the trees. I have always been interested in old graveyards. The stories of people who had gone before, the sense of time, our own lives only adding to a longer thread. On every grave, dates and times, a person's life reduced and preserved in a few words. A last clutch at immortality. Perhaps I deviated from the path, but suddenly

I stumbled and fell to my knees in the long grass. I clutched at a low tombstone to right myself. It was cold and rough to my touch and I looked a little closer. It was a simple slab of Hawkesbury sandstone. Cracked and speckled with lichen in its shady place, it stood a little apart from the others with rank grass between, its inscription eroded almost to illegibility.

On my knees for a moment, I looked closer and read the faint message:

Here lies Michael Ryan.
Born - 1810. Died - In punishment
1838. R.I.P.

As I pushed myself up, I paused to consider this poor young man. What awful crime had provoked his final punishment? He may have earned his memorial but he died far from his family and friends. Perhaps it was imagination, yet I felt that my touch on the stone had formed a bond with Mr. Ryan. I shivered briefly and tried to find a more pleasant mood though I could not shake the feeling that Michael Ryan was still with me as I stumbled on towards the church. The feeling did not leave me until I reached the path. I was reassured by the better footing but the incident left me feeling strangely unsettled. I tried to put it out of my mind.

Mr. Reynolds, the verger was a tall cadaverous fellow of serious demeanor and receding white hair, the sort of person who's always relaxed and content with his position. He was polishing some sort of plate in the nave when I found him. I tried to mention the incident in the cemetery and he listened with a polite smile but it was soon clear he hadn't felt anything unusual in his years in the church so I didn't discuss it further.

'Here's a key to the vestry door,' he said in a soft voice, frowning as he produced an ancient-looking iron key on a large ring. I immediately had images of cartoon jailers and manacled prisoners.

'There's a jug if you want to make a cup of tea, make sure you wash any cups you use.' He clearly had ideas about the habits of tradesmen.

'How long can I stay?'

'We don't need the room till next Monday, so you can stay as long as you like. Just make sure you leave the room in a clean state as Mrs. Edwards won't be in until Wednesday.'

'Can you tell me a little about the building?' I asked as he moved towards the door.

'He turned and looked at me, his eyebrows arching in surprise.

'Oh,' he said turning back. 'It was part of the old Church, St. Mathews, built in 1815 ... ' His face was animated. I had clearly touched on a genuine area of interest in the fellow.

'Are you interested in church history?' he asked.

'Well, I'm interested in historic architecture, and I like to know about the buildings I work on. They were wonderful builders, you know? They did amazing things with little more than broken stones and burnt sea shells.'

'Yes, I'm sure,' he said, turning back to the door. Clearly his fondness for history did not extend to technicalities.

He led me out the door and over to the vestry and showed me where the work was to be done. It wasn't much, just a few patches of delaminated plaster near the skirting, a common problem that I'd seen before. It would've been easy to make a cosmetic repair but I had been hired for restoration work. I needed to match the work of long dead tradesmen as well as the rather bland appearance of the wall.

The next week, late one summer's day; a Friday I remember, I let myself into the deserted building through the side door.

Although it was late afternoon the sharp summer sun cast strong shadows in the yard. I stepped over the slate step and pushed aside the heavy wooden door. It was then that I felt a chill and the light seemed to suddenly fade as though I had entered a dark and gloomy forest. I stopped, feeling very uncertain for reasons I could not explain to myself. I put it down to my imagination and carried on with the preparations for my work. The high stained glass windows gave little relief from the gloom so, after a time, I looked for a light to better illuminate the area. Finding none, I returned to my car and rummaged around for the old camping lantern I sometimes used, returned to the rectory and set out my tools and materials on a trestle table I found in the corner of a bedroom. My preparations complete, I settled down to the task at hand.

The job wasn't difficult, just very detailed; the old plaster, as fragile as an old man's skin, held together by a hard coat of paint. It broke and bled fine sand and mortar as soon as I touched it. I had to carefully match my compounds to the original work and gently work my trowel so as not to damage more than I repaired.

I thought of the original tradesmen - doubtless convicts, perhaps Michael Ryan numbering in their ranks; and how much they'd achieved so long ago.

The age of the building pressed on me. During such tough times for everyone, the church must've seemed like a haven to many.

Yet as a local boy, I knew Samuel Marsden, the infamous "flogging parson", had died in this very building. I wondered whether he'd ever regretted any of his judgments or whether he'd ever doubted redemption by the lash-and-the-book was even possible as he returned to the house from his day in the Parramatta courts, to take off his robes and hang them…there … near the door …perhaps.

Slowly the cracks and scuffs of time responded to my attention. Oblivious to everything, my hands worked through long practice as though by some automatic process. Time passed and the pale light faded from the high windows.

I worked slowly and intently, hunched in my haven of light surrounded by darkness that grew ever deeper. The odd sounds in the dusty timbers, the occasional creaking of the roof as it cooled from the summer sun, or the soft brush of a tree branch against the wall did not disturb me. Absorbed in my work, my thoughts drifted to the wretched men and boys who had done this work. I pictured myself kneeling awkwardly in leg irons applying a trowel to this wall. I wondered about the pain and suffering of the convicts, how they lived, the isolation and lonely despair they must have felt.…

A sudden chill stilled my hand and I knew I was not alone.. Though I didn't turn around, I knew that someone was behind me, watching. A presence that I could not deny. I slowly turned, convinced that someone, perhaps the verger, had entered unnoticed and was here with me, but no soul appeared within the limit of my lantern light. The chill passed quickly but the conviction remained.

I returned to my work with considerable unease, unable to shake the feeling of dread and terrible loneliness.

My heart pounding and with thoughts of a dignified escape filling my mind, I was readying to stop work and resume the next day when I noticed it: a tiny corner of yellowed paper peeping out from the crack between the floor and the skirting. To this day I can't say why such a minor thing would interrupt my thoughts of escape, yet it did.

The chill returned with a sudden draught as I pulled the paper free, my breath coming in short bursts as I held it in my palm as though if might crumble into pieces at the slightest movement.

The paper was yellow and crisp with age; and about the size of my palm. The rough edges suggested it'd been torn from a book or journal; the faded writing difficult to make out, its style crude and uneven. I stared intently as though I could somehow divine the meaning by imprinting it on my brain; making out a few letters, then a word, yes, "lashes" and "died in punishment."

I pictured the poor soul slumped at the triangle, his back shredded by the lash, and, as I did, the hovering presence left.

I felt a great loss, like the death of someone close.

The door rattled and a warm draught began.

'Is anyone there?' enquired a voice.

Steve looked at me sharply when I finished speaking. Perhaps he did not believe me.

We've only met a few times since and we never discuss the old rectory.

Perhaps he thinks me a bit strange; he could be right.

I would never sell the scrap of paper or anything. I keep it safe at home and I never mention it to anyone.

It's now a private matter between me and Michael.

River of Lies

In Deep Water

At precisely 12.55am, Brian pushed open the battered door of *The Old Boatshed*. The place was a dark cave, a single space with an empty dance floor at one end and a bar, a harbour of light, at the other.

Raucous music assaulted his ears and the fetid air irritated his throat, but he forced himself forward past dim tables and pale faces. Vague nautical artifacts decorated the walls with crossed oars, coils of rope and fishing nets.

He reached the bar and considered making enquiries from the barman, then dismissed the idea and ordered a beer. The barman made change for his $100 note, without comment.

By 1:00am precisely Brian was straddling a barstool shaped like an old barrel. *And just as comfortable*, he thought. His right hand fondled his beer while in his left he held the pink envelope like a banner. He felt like a cat protecting an old fish carcass and imagined hungry cat's eyes regarding him from the surrounding gloom.

What would they see? A man not yet middle-aged yet afraid of life slipping by; a pale face and blue eyes below a cap of brown hair, short and spiked; jeans and jacket plucked from the young men's rack.

The bar mirror did not lie.

Life was slipping past.

Enough, this mystery would be a new beginning; a chance to restart his life. He pulled himself back to the present and looked past the bottles and nautical knickknacks framing the mirror. If Leticia were here, she would not fail to see him, nor the envelope. He sipped his beer slowly while his mind tried to make sense of it all.

It had started with an innocent visit to the library. All he wanted was a few pointers on fly-casting: his current passion. Then as he searched the rows of books, the bound copy of Death on the Nile next to The Complete Angler was like a Royal Coachman fly to a hungry salmon. His stubby fingers were pulling the book from the shelf even as his imagination leapt ahead.

He knew of people who would hide a book they fancied among other less attractive volumes. It was common practice among law students, or so he'd been told. But this was a public library. Who would want dibs on a detective story? Perhaps it was a particularly good read. He'd barely time to open the volume when a thick envelope fell from its pages, postcard size and an awful shade of teenage pink. Putting aside Mrs. Christie for the moment, Brian picked it up. His searching fingers quickly extracted the contents: five green pristine $100 notes; and a single sheet of paper.

"Meet me at the old boatshed at 1.00am. Leticia",

written in black ink and with the flourish of a feminine hand.

So here he was, way past his bedtime and feeling foolish. An ersatz detective in a budget movie!

Lost in the corners of his mind, the cooking show on the TV behind the bar flickered without sound, vague images of carrots and talking heads. It was some time before he realised his beer glass was empty.

Shadowy figures slipped past unnoticed.

The bar lights dimmed.

A late straggler emerged from the ladies toilet and headed for the street. Time to go! What a fool he'd been. It was clear now "the old boatshed" could have meant any one of the hundreds of old boatsheds on the river, of which only one was known to Leticia and the intended recipient of the note and money. How smart he had been to think of the bar by that name, and how wrong.

'Follow me you fool, if you want to live!'

The words delivered in a husky whisper shattered his reverie. He jerked erect, almost dropping the envelope. He regained his grasp on the situation in sufficient time to see a slim female figure disappear through the barroom door and onto the street; his shocked, *"what, who?"* delivered to an empty room as he lunged toward the door in pursuit.

She, whoever she was, had disappeared.

The street was empty apart from a few darkened cars parked nearby.

'Get in, quickly!' sounded a now-familiar voice.

A condemned man about to meet his executioner, Brian slipped into the dark interior of the waiting car. The closing door sounded like a falling guillotine.

The upholstery smelled of old farts and cigarette smoke, but the hooded figure beside him challenged these with aromas of Jasmine and beer. He had no time to consider the contradictions before she spoke.

'Who are you; and what do you want?'

Brian judged the speaker to be young and angry. Her accent told him nothing.

"Are you Leticia? We finally meet. But, you're being a little overdramatic you know." In the front seat, the driver's face, revealed in the dashboard's glare, was broad and dark.

"Shut up! You have no idea what you've got yourself into, have you? I can't figure out whether you're very dumb or something else." She crowded into the other corner of the seat to face him squarely the hood drawn across her face.

'Book theft is a crime, you know?' said Brian.

She did not reply immediately, and then her low laugh surprised him. He managed to glimpse a small nose framed by light brown hair as the vehicle turned at a well-lit intersection. 'Just as I thought: stupid! OK, just give me the money and the note and Abbas will let you out. We'll say no more about it.'

'Now you're the one being silly. That note is as good as a confession to whatever you've done, or are doing. And besides, I don't have it on me,' he lied. 'It's in a safe place, though. Tell me what's going on or I'll go to the police."

There was a pause, a sigh as she turned her head away.

She spoke a short clipped sentence in a language Brian did not understand as the car turned towards the river.

As they moved beyond street lights and buildings, Brian realised he was no closer to solving the mystery connected to Death on the Nile. Perhaps it was more than some frivolous game. The appearance of Abbas and the foreign connection seemed to suggest something more complex, more serious. He was about to speak, to perhaps restart negotiations, when the car tyres crunched on gravel, then something smoother.

A few solitary stars glowed like moth holes in a shroud.

'What's going on?' he shouted. The car stopped abruptly. Abbas swung in his seat, pointed a large pistol at Brian's head and cocked it with a thick thumb.

'Get out of car, slowly,' he said with a thick accent.

Brian did as he was told.

They'd stopped at the old landing. Last century the area bustled with shipments of logs and wool. Now it was deserted except for their car and a killer with a large pistol. Five metres below, the water ran smoothly in moonlit tranquility.

Brian did not wait for Abbas to exit the car, he ran. He ran into the dim moonlight as he had not run before. No need to dodge and weave, his stumbling steps made a difficult target.

A low explosion - a puff of gases - before something pulled at the loose cloth below his armpit.

A silencer, for God sake!

They really were trying to kill him!

With a final lurch, he launched himself into the river.

The dark water closed over him like a suit of armour, welcoming, protecting, not to be feared but enjoyed. The water seemed to drag him down but he kicked off his shoes, freed himself from his waterlogged coat and surfaced under the landing.

The darkness was absolute. He could only tell the edge of heavy timbers above by the absence of stars. His groping fingers found a post and held its rough surface while he regained his breath, listening.

At first, silence; then a faint sound far above!

The scuff of a shoe!

Someone waiting!

Silence roared in his ears and he began to shiver. A car horn delivered a single sharp sound. Footsteps started up and led quickly off towards the road.

Midstream

"'I tell you, Inspector, they tried to kill me.'

Brian tried to keep his voice calm.

'Are you sure it wasn't just some sort of practical joke, Mr. Edwards?' said Inspector Schilling; his flat voice revealing no emotion as his dark eyes regarded Brian.

'I know when I'm being shot at. Find my coat and you'll find a bullet hole in it!'

'The officers who picked you up at the landing reported you were dripping wet, no coat or shoes and that you smelled of beer. You were drinking, perhaps, when you lost this note and money?'

'Yes!'

The telephone on the desk gave a short chirp.

Schilling picked it up and listened.

'Yeah, OK,' he said.

He replaced the receiver and turned back to Brian.

'Let's go back to the beginning. You went to the library yesterday to get a book and you found an envelope with $500 in it.'

'Yes, I've told you that,' said Brian, putting a definite edge on his voice.

'Why didn't you report it to the librarian, Mr. Edwards? Did you intend to keep the money?'

'Err, well … no. I thought the message was suspicious, so I decided to investigate further.'

'So you went to … let me see, *The Old Boatshed* bar to find the writer of the note.'

'Yes.'

'Were you going to ask them for more money?'

'No, of course not!'

'What then? If you had suspicions, why didn't you report the matter to the police?'

'I was just curious, Inspector. I just wanted to know what it was all about.'

'I see. So this curiosity means someone says something and you get into the back of a strange car?'

'"Yeah ... well...'

A loud knock sounded on the door and a tall man in a grey suit entered without invitation. He smiled at Brian, and Inspector Schilling, and found a chair, his brown features falling into a frown of concentration as his blue eyes regarded Brian closely.

'This is Detective Lambert from our Police Intelligence Unit,' Schilling said, grim faced.

Lambert lent forward, smiling; and shook Brian's hand. His grip was firm, but brief.

'Yes, we do have some intelligence in the Force; though don't always show it, Mr. Edwards!'

It was clearly an old joke told with brevity.

Brian relaxed a little.

'We believe your experience could be linked to one of our on-going investigations; and a recent death,' he continued, glancing quickly at Inspector Schilling.

'I can't tell you much, but ... let's just say there appears to be a connection between a man's body found in the river a few days ago, *The Old Boatshed* bar and the library. We think they are parts of a larger case involving millions of dollars.'

'There's no need for details, Detective,' began Inspector Schilling, 'I'm sure Mr. Edwards does not want to know how we operate.' He shuffled papers and rested his elbows on the desk.

Brian lent back, clearly his little mystery was part of something decidedly bigger. If he waited and listened what else would be revealed?

'I don't think it does any harm to give Mr. Edwards more information. He has already suffered in this case and deserves to know what's going on.' Lambert looked at Brian as he spoke, though his words were clearly directed at the Inspector.

'The fact is, Mr. Edwards, the body found in the river was that of an undercover policeman, a colleague of ours, so the department is very anxious to find his killers, as you can well appreciate.' Inspector Schilling stared at him with open hostility before Detective Lambert paused, for a moment. 'Your little adventure has been very useful in flushing out fresh information on this case but we would like you to do one more thing to help us.'

'What is that?' Brian managed to croak, his mouth dry.

'We want you to go back to The Old Boatshed," said Detective Lambert.

During the day, The Old Boatshed was just another dingy bar. The nautical artifacts looked out of place and the western music better suited to another era. The place was deserted except for an old man in the corner who regarded Brian with rheumy curiosity. This barman was a young black man, a stranger to Brian, and showed no recognition as he approached.

'A lemon, lime and soda, please,' said Brian to the other's unasked question.

The next move, Brian knew, was to ask to speak to Leticia, yet he hesitated. The microphone in his jacket was well hidden, but the listeners at police headquarters would not expect Leticia to appear straightaway and so put herself at risk.

He took a deep breath and tried to relax, tried to look more like a midday drinker. If the barman noticed his nervousness, he made no comment as he busied himself arranging bottles.

The telephone behind the bar gave a discreet buzz. The barman lifted the handset and listened for a few seconds then gave a shrug and handed it across the bar to a querying Brian. 'How would I know!' he said in response to Brian's raised eyebrow.

'Hello Mr. Andrews. What do you want? Wasn't one near miss enough for you?' Her voice sounded thin and distant.

'Where are you; and what are you up to?' managed Brian, squeezing his words through a dry throat.

'Go home and forget us or we may be forced to try again. We know you're working with the police now. We can find you at any time.'

Brian drew a deep breath and opened his mouth to answer but a click sounded and the line went dead.

'Is everything OK?' enquired the barman.

Brian's pale face and open mouth could not be ignored.

'Yeah, yeah, sure, just bad news,' he mumbled as he turned and stumbled to the door.

'Well that was a waste of time!' said Inspector Schilling as his face showed his contempt for the plan.

'I don't know what else I could have done,' said Brian. 'Perhaps I'm not cut out for this "cloak-and-dagger stuff."'

'You did fine, Brian,' offered Detective Lambert. 'We've had our fears confirmed.'

'Oh, yeah! How's that?'

Schilling's mouth curled in disdain. Lambert paused, and spoke again. 'The message Brian found at the library must've been placed within minutes of when it was expected to be collected.'

'How does that help anything?' said Inspector Schilling, tapping the table impatiently with his fingertips.

Lambert ignored the interruption. 'The library has a very good CCTV security system. We looked at all the footage for the time Brian was at the library. We found Brian of course, but we also found video of someone we know. His name is Tony Shevlin, one of the suspects in the case. He's employed as a scheduler in a small shipping company, but we believe he is also a partner in the smuggling operation.'

'What about the other person? This "Leticia", the person who placed the note and money,' said Brian.

Lambert's voice dropped to a lower tone and his face adopted a serious expression.

'Yes, we did find one other person … a police clerk. We think he's been selling information. That's why Leticia said, "We know you're working with the police now." There will be an enquiry of course,' he said, looking at Inspector Schilling, 'but we won't arrest him as yet, if that's OK with you Inspector.'

Inspector Schilling nodded dumbly.

'And, one other thing! We've been tapping Tony Shevlin's phone. The *SS Bangkok* from Hong Kong-via-Jakarta arrives tomorrow and we expect it will be carrying more of the … contraband.'

'And what exactly, is that?' asked Brian in frustration.

'People, Brian. They're smuggling people,' said Detective Lambert as he rose and headed to the door.

Muddy Waters

Light escaping weakly below the bathroom door was enough to show Brian the writing desk, mini-bar and bare details of his narrow bed while the rest of the room lay in dark shadows. He was safe here he knew, yet he was still unable to sleep. The events of the day tumbled through his head, engaging him in relentless internal dialogue. He'd dismissed sleep long ago. Something was wrong! It was all too simple: ship arrives, police swoop, criminals captured, case over. However, Leticia was far from stupid! Even after months of investigation, her identity remained a mystery. Sure, some progress had been made, but only a few minor players had been identified and if they were arrested, Leticia could still escape.

He realised the adventure was over.

The case now dominated his life and he was afraid to sleep at his own home.

There was no fun left, only the possibility of death.

This possibility did not scare him greatly, he'd faced death before, but he much preferred the continuing fascination of life. He was pleased for the first time that he had no family to worry about yet he could not stay hidden. It would not be over until the ringleader was caught and the case closed.

Who was Leticia?

Where did she live?

How did she run the smuggling operation?

A thought lingered on the edge of his consciousness though it skittered and ducked when he tried to concentrate. *Leticia … Leticia …* then, between one thought and the next, sleep claimed him.

A shaft of bright sunlight found a gap in the heavy curtains and crossed the room. Brian lay for a while in drowsy pleasure until driven to the bathroom. Returning to the single room, he began to prepare his breakfast on the small bench. Orange juice, muesli and a cup of tea would lift his spirits. The day promised to be bright and sunny thought he carried a cloud he could not shake.

Between the orange juice and the muesli, he realised what had been worrying him about the case, and about Leticia. She was invisible; perhaps the incident in the car a regrettable aberration. He doubted Shevlin, the police informer - perhaps even Abbas - had any idea of who she really was.

Yet she sat in the middle of a huge people smuggling operation and had never been photographed, or recorded anywhere. *How could that be? How could she manage her gang; she must communicate with at least two groups: the smugglers and the distributers, to coordinate the operation?*

He picked up his mobile phone and texted Detective Lambert on the number he'd been given.

Any news on SS Bangkok?

The answer came almost immediately.

Unloading regular cargo now. Waiting. What about coffee? You know where.

Sure, 20 mins.

The café was a small building where the river road met the edge of a small park. Once it had been a workers cottage, now it found new life serving the idle middle class. The open lawns of the park swept down to the water's edge and a few isolated trees dressed the landscape. Lambert had pointed it out as they passed on the way to The Old Boatshed the day before; and Brian noted the wisdom of the detective's choice. Although noisy from passing traffic, the place was open and exposed. There was no chance of a sneak attack here. Lambert was already seated at a small table in the morning sun.

'G'day, Brian, how did you sleep?' Brian again noticed how the detective's breezy attitude could put him at ease.

'Not very well actually,' said Brian. They both ordered cappuccinos-in-a-mug and Brian related his latest ruminations. He'd just reached the subject of Leticia's communication system when they were interrupted. Brian saw the detective's mouth drop open and his eyes widen as he looked over Brian's shoulder to the road.

The warning and the noise came almost simultaneously.

'Look out!' and the sound of a motorcycle revving loudly. The table crashed over and somehow he was behind it as the rapid tuck-tuck-tuck of a machine pistol shattered the morning. As Brian crouched the insane screaming of the motorcycle faded in the distance.

Silence, now somehow more intense, reclaimed the day.

Detective Lambert was already on his phone describing the motorcycle and its riders as Brian picked himself up and flopped onto a chair. The acrid smell of cordite hung in the air.

By the time the police had taken his statement and the ordered crowd of emergency workers dispersed, Brian had come to a conclusion. He'd go back to the beginning and see if anything had been missed. The attack at the café was the last straw. The police were doing their best, but he would get no rest until Leticia and all those about her were arrested.

He bought a limp hamburger and a plastic bottle of orange juice and sat by the water. Nothing seemed out of place. Life on the river went on oblivious to his petty concerns. Timber lighters and other small craft filled the foreground while in the distance several larger boats felt their careful way between the mud shoals bordering the channel. He finished his orange juice and was considering whether to attempt the last of the hamburger, when his phone rang. It was Detective Lambert.

'The illegals were in two specially adapted containers covered with normal cargo. They weren't hard to find. We watched them loaded onto trucks and stopped them outside the gates. There were 63 in all, mostly men, with a handful of women and children.'

'What about the gang?'

'Yeah, we made three arrests, two are in hospital with wounds, but they don't know much. We sent the empty containers on to the next staging point. Maybe we can pick up a few more if they haven't been tipped off,' said Lambert though to Brian's ear he didn't sound hopeful.

'Congratulations on the raid, but it doesn't sound like progress. I think I'll spend the rest of the afternoon at the library. Perhaps I'll find something to read.'

'Leave any questions to the police, Brian.' Advised Lambert as he rang off.

Leticia had organised it all very well. Each individual in the organisation knew his job and nothing more; she was isolated, protected. If he wanted to see the end of this, she had to be found, and neutralised.

The seagulls accepted the remains of his Big Mac with noisy bickering as Brian pointed his hire car towards the library. He could think of two reasons to start there: One. it was where the whole story began; and Two … he had no other ideas.

It was late in the afternoon when he arrived. The imposing building was a legacy from an earlier mayor, a landmark in the town and considered the best library in the State. He walked to the adult non-fiction section and scanned the rows of books. The section on fly-fishing was as it was before. He noticed several books he'd previously borrowed were in their rightful places. *Indexed and arranged like weapons in a battle against ignorance.* Of course Death on the Nile was not among them as he expected, nor were there any other out-of-place books.

He cast his eyes on the books and shelves. *What was he missing?* The mystery started here. It involved ships and people smuggling, the exchange of messages and even an informant at police headquarters. The library CCTV security camera had been very useful in finding two involved individuals, perhaps there were more! On an impulse, he left the dim alleyways of Adult Non-fiction and made his way to the front desk. Three young library staff worked shoulder to shoulder, checking out books from the motley crowd of last minute borrowers.

He approached the nearest.

'Could I see the Library Director, please?' he asked as she turned to him smiling.

'Oh, do you have a complaint?' she asked shortly, a frown of resentment distorting her face.

'No, no, it's another matter; it's important,' he said seriously.

'Oh, very well sir. I'll see. She is usually very busy at this time. What name shall I say?' she said as she snatched up the phone and punched several keys.

'Andrews, Brian Andrews.'

'Excuse me, Miss Grisham, a Mr. Andrews is here. He wants to speak to you.' Her face draped in doubt, 'It's important ...he says.'

Silence dragged for several seconds before the girl opened her mouth to speak again, listened, then put down the telephone.

'Miss Grisham will see you,' she said with obvious surprise. 'Take the lift to the third floor.'

She turned away and began gathering her belongings as her companions dealt with the last of the borrowers.

Brian followed directions while steaming inwardly at the arrogance of civil servants who happily took the public's pay cheque while wallowing in idle self-importance. *All this for a few hours of CCTV.* Maybe he should give "Miss Grisham" his lecture on public service.

A Fall from Aloft

The lift door slid open on a small foyer with river themed wallpaper, pot plants and a single cedar panelled door. Brian turned the knob and entered without knocking, still steaming at his treatment at the front desk.

'Good afternoon, Mr. Andrews,'

Miss Grisham was a slim young woman in a severe business suit; her disarming voice was young and cultivated with rounded vowels and crisp sibilants. A stage voice, like a well made dress, Brian thought, with a puzzling undertone of mockery.

She rose from her seat at a large glass-topped desk across an expanse of deep pile carpet, and came to meet him. Behind her, a window displayed the setting sun behind glowing clouds. The river shone below, spread like a silver plain among hills of shadow. Brian strode forward holding out his hand.

'Thank you for seeing me, Miss Grisham. My name's Brian Andrews. What a wonderful ... ,'' he stopped in mid-sentence his mind still processing the scene, the situation, the woman he faced. A primitive part of his brain cried, 'Danger!' and the flight reflex cut in without engaging his conscious mind. He was turning to flee as she spoke.

'Yes, Mr. Andrews. I see you know me now, and I know you haven't told anyone ...'

Brian completed the turn. Too late, Abbas stood by the door, looking ridiculously short though his broad frame spread like a wall across the doorway, a pistol at his side, the silencer fitted and raised as Brian backed away.

'You've already met Abbas,' she said from behind him. 'He is quite anxious to make up for his previous failures, you know,' her voice was high and tone disdainful. She was enjoying the moment.

'Why did you have to be so good looking? I just knew that you had to be trouble. You have no idea ..,' Brian kept backing from Abbas's levelled gun, his face a picture of panic. Laughing, Leticia raised her hands to ward off his alarmed backward steps. Too late, she realised her mistake.

As her hands touched his back Brian turned in one swift movement, took her wrists and swung her body like a shield. The sound of the pistol shot was drowned by her shriek. The scene moved in silent slow motion. Abbas hesitated, unsure where to aim. Brian heard only his own heavy breathing as he slowly released the dead weight in his arms. Then Abbas raised the gun again, his face a mask of indecision, as the door was flung violently open.

'Drop the weapon, Andre Abbas, you're under arrest.' said Detective Lambert. Abbas turned to face the new danger the gun still levelled, but Lambert stepped close and held his automatic to the killer's head. There was no need for words. Abbas allowed the silenced pistol to be taken from his limp fingers as his shoulders slumped in defeat.

The office was suddenly crowded with uniforms and grey suits. Detective Lambert stood calmly by the door issuing orders and taking reports from junior officers. His tall figure seemed to be the centre of a maelstrom around which all other activities revolved. Inspector Schilling to one side appeared an operatic figure in silver buttons and braided cap. Abbas was nowhere to be seen.

As the room was searched, a partition was swung aside to reveal a bank of TV monitors and telephone handsets facing a single high-backed chair. An officer with a lap top computer inserted a lead and began tapping on a keyboard.

Brian knelt beside the crumpled figure on the floor. Her dark suit no longer seemed so severe and her delicate features still wore an expression of surprise. A crimson river spoiled the pristine beauty of the carpet. He noticed for the first time how small and delicate she seemed. A paramedic shook his head at his silent question. Brian took her hand in his as her green eyes shut for a moment then opened.

'Leticia, hang on ...'

'Not Leticia, Mr. Andrews. Diana, call me Diana, I ...'

Her voice was like a feather on water caught between tides as she shut her eyes, her expression faded and life flowed from her.

End of the Road

The road from the ridge ran in a swoop to the water's edge and disappeared below the brown flood, a watery blanket covering the landscape and stretching to the horizon. Above the surface there was no sign of the road. Ryan didn't know where it ended, did not care.

Wheels skidded as he backed the truck down to the water and switched off the motor. The rhythmic swish of wipers died and a rapid tattoo of rain on the hood replaced the motor's roar. Ryan liked the rain and grey sky; memories of safety and a warm bed, *a place to hide.*

Breaking off the thought, he wiped away lank hair, reached for his hat and stepped down from the cab into the deluge. Water cascaded from his coat and drummed on his hat as he squelched through rivulets of water scouring the yellow clay of the road. At the rear of the truck, he fumbled with the wet rope canvas lashings. The green tarpaulin once belonged to a farmer in Deniliquin, *a simple thing to slip in with a few hay bales while he worked on the farm.*

He chuckled as his fingers worked to uncover a small dinghy. He dragged it quickly to the end of the tray and eased the stern onto the mud. A small outboard motor and oars followed. He worried about the noise of the outboard, but decided it was worth the risk. Anyway, the rain would swallow the noise as surely as lamp light in a fog. The dinghy left a ragged groove in the mud as he dragged it nearer the rapidly rising flood line.

No point in advertising his presence. According to the radio, rescue teams had already swept this area and helicopters were unlikely to be flying this late in the afternoon, still it was better to be careful.

He walked to the truck and swung his stocky frame into the driver's seat. The wheels spun, found purchase and he drove the vehicle beneath the spreading branches of a large gum, out of sight. *He could use a bit of help with this work*. But most of the people he could trust were far away, or still in prison. And that would mean splitting the profits, anyway.

He walked back to the dinghy.

This was the fifth house he'd raided this week and he knew the routine. The pickings were good yet he needed to be quick to beat the rising water. In a couple of hours, he'd be back in town and no one would know where he'd been. A self-satisfied smile creased his face as he wiped errant raindrops from his chin.

He launched the dinghy with practiced ease and started the motor. The small boat pushed resolutely across the rushing stream and the grey surface slid past in pockmarked turmoil. The only gauge of distance in the driving screen of water was the occasional tree poking its crown above the surface like a drowning man, swaying in sympathy with the violent current below. At several points, Ryan deviated to avoid flotsam that charged at the boat. Whole trees, ripped from the waterlogged soil appeared and disappeared in the gloom. On one, a wide-eyed rabbit hopped back and forth, lonely captain of a giant grey-gum log. *It should be thankful.* It had a chance of survival, no matter how small. Rabbits were survivors like him. He would survive too; he would show them who was smart.

The rain beat in endless torment against his face. He sat numbly in a world of his own, all outside noise obscured by the scream of the outboard. He blinked into the deluge and began to worry he might've missed the house, yet suddenly the tops of two large alien pines appeared above the water on the left side of the boat. He swung the bow to pass between the trees, once markers of the front gate of the homestead. He could picture the layout; remembered from a few days' work on the farm the winter before. The roads, the cattle yards and barn were all under water. The farm machinery and vehicles were gone. There was no sign of the dusty patch of front garden the farmer's wife struggled to maintain. The only sign of the rambling old timber house was the white second floor with a green iron roof, a television antenna canted incongruously from one corner; a strange island alone on a grey ocean.

He eyed the building with distaste-mingled-with satisfaction. That fool Evans shouldn't have sacked him and Stevie Price last winter! Doubtless the old farmer and his wife climbed to the top floor to escape the floods. How ironic their rescue made his job easy.

He reduced speed and steered the boat slightly up stream as he approached the house. The current sucked at the corners of the building causing ripples and little whirlpools, forming and breaking away in the stream only to be replaced and disappear again. On the downstream side, he found a small balcony not yet covered by the water, though it lapped at its edges. *This must be the main bedroom; could even be dry inside, but not for long.*

He'd have half an hour at the most to find anything valuable, if the old house lasted that long! He tied the dinghy to the balcony, checked his backpack, and scrambled over the rail. Abandoned clothing inside the sliding door confirmed the owners' hasty escape. *Of course, the idiots would take papers and family photographs first and leave money and other valuables behind, always the same, sentimental fools.*

He thanked them silently for their stupidity.

The room was just as he'd imagined: steep timber rafters ascending to a central roof beam; a door at the far end, probably a toilet. No water showed through the polished timber floorboards, yet he would need to hurry. The floor shuddered as he moved to the nearest bureau and clawed at the top drawer: women's clothing; the same in the other drawers. As he turned to the second chest of drawers, the shudder increased. Something heavy struck the house. A loud crash, followed by a scraping noise that continued for long seconds, then stopped.

He threw clothes about furiously.

Still nothing!

Only the built-in wardrobe and bathroom remained. He flung open the wardrobe doors in frustration. At last, a low bench on one side with drawers below. The top drawer yielded nothing of interest. Neither did the second. In the third drawer, he had more luck: a small camera in a soft bag. He shoved it quickly into his backpack and opened the last drawer.

Finally success!

A heavy steel cash box, still locked!

They obviously intended to return.

As he touched the box, the house gave another violent shudder. With frantic haste, he stuffed it into his backpack and swung it onto his back. He turned and lunged for the door just as the floor lurched and canted upwards on one side. Water rushed into the lower end of the room. Through the open door, he glimpsed the dinghy rope tugging at the landing rail. He tried to run but slipped on the sloping floor and fell to his knees. A groan sounded above, timber torn from timber; the ceiling beam, released at one end from the wall, pivoted towards him. The chest of drawers he'd recently searched slid across the floor towards him, striking him squarely in the chest, and pinning him against the wardrobe. Mouth open in horror he watched as the beam continued it's slow decent and lodged on the chest of drawers. In rising panic, he pushed against the tangle of furniture and wood; the house—now a jumble of irregular planes and splintered timber—returned to its quiet shuddering.

He screamed for help and reached towards the door, a screech of nails, ripping from wood; and the landing rail, broke away from its posts.

He'd time to see the dinghy disappear from sight when he felt water at his neck, then at his chin.

The rain continued for the rest of the day.

And throughout the night.

In the morning, it stopped and a bleak sun rose over a vast expanse of grey water. Helicopter crews hurrying to more urgent areas, noted the house could no longer be seen.

No Rest for Alec

**The** light was fading fast as Alec climbed the hill and searched for the road the old man had described. He didn't have a great choice of turns. Cobbled streets abutted leafy lanes and the estates of the wealthy in this part of the village. Another few minutes and he would be in the country again.

It had been a long but rewarding walk from yesterday's hostel. He felt like a man reborn, all worries of recent times left in the city as he looked forward to the open road and new discoveries.

Afterwards he would blame brashness and the failing light for his mistake. Now he confidently turned into the first street on the left.

The sign read, "Gallows Lane," or at least he thought it did. With the full faith of the ignorant, he quickened his pace. Perhaps there would still be time for supper.

As though recognising the impending end of the journey, his limbs began to ache; muscles not earlier noticed began to protest. His large pack appeared ridiculously over-loaded. The band of his wide-brimmed hat cut maliciously into his forehead.

As he made the turn, the remaining light faded to a few flashes of lightning on the southern horizon. In a distant copse, an owl hooted.

A large building loomed on his left, barely visible in the gloom. It seemed to beetle overhead as he approached at an oblique angle. Strange, he'd not expected a large place. The U-pub website made it sound small and intimate. He made a mental note to rate the site ★★★☆☆.

He judged he was now in front of the house so looked for a path to the door, eventually choosing a section of the grey foreground slightly lighter than the deeper shadows on either side. With a surge of annoyance, he decided he'd complain to his host at the first opportunity. Surely, any decent hostel could afford a sign and a lighted walkway? He could not be the first guest to arrive on foot after sunset.

He pushed between bushes bordering what might've been rusted iron gates; and counted his good fortune when his feet found a gravel path. The crunching of his boots was reassuring and now he could just make out the building against the lighter overcast sky. Lightning continued to flash on the horizon, the sound of thunder faint.

He felt the first few drops of rain as something large and dark fluttered briefly overhead.

What now, bats?

I hate bats! Suddenly chilled, he hurried his steps to a stone portico wide enough for a hansom cab, remnant of a bygone age. A misty vision of a couple, in crinoline and top hat, arose and as quickly faded from his imagination.

The rain descended in earnest as he hurried undercover. White marble steps appeared to glow in the gloom, leading arrivals upward to two tall oak doors set into the black face of the building. No liveried footman emerged to assist Alec as he left his muddy boot prints on the stone.

He thumped on the huge doors in the dark, his fumbling efforts finally revealing an ancient bell chain. At his pull, a faint clang sounded hollowly from deep within the building. Relieved, he unslung his pack and waited.

Coldness, long kept at bay by the strenuous walk, now began to enfold him.

Pacing did not alleviate the chill or his impatience. He considered alternatives, the local pub perhaps. He was about to turn away when scraping sounds from the other side of the door suggested that heavy bolts were being withdrawn.

Finally, the door swung open and a tall figure appeared. He held a large candelabrum on which three candles guttered fiercely as he thrust it at Alec's face. This was certainly the strangest person Alec had encountered for some time. He was dressed in black with a white cravat, ruffled sleeves and leggings, but his most striking features were his hairless head and deathly white painted face. His lips were red and his eyes were as two orange embers at the bottom of dark pits.

The remarkable creature fixed Alec with blazing eyes and opened his red-rimmed mouth, drawing it back in what he may have imagined was a smile and exposing two enormous fangs that would have made Dracula proud.

'Can I be of athithstance to you, sir?' he voiced with a theatrical bow.

'I'm expected. My name's Alec.'

Said Alec impatiently, pushing forward.

"The Mathter will be delighted," lisped the strange apparition stepping back, "he ith at the back with the otherth. But where ith your cothstume and thteak for the barbie?"

There would be no rest for Alec tonight.

Fatal Voyage

From the bridge deck Pearson could see almost the full length of the ship. At the bow an occasional flurry of spray appeared briefly before being snatched away by a brisk northeast breeze. Long rollers ran deeply across the grey-green sea and chased the wind to the horizon. The deck barely moved.

Amazing how stable 100,000 tonnes of oil can feel, marvelled Pearson. He turned back to the man by his side.

'Have you got statements from the crew yet, Owens?'

'I've spoken to everyone, Boss. A few have alibis, if they can be trusted. The Second Officer and one seaman were on the bridge, and the Engineer and Chief Steward were playing cards together. The captain, the cook and the other seaman claim to have been resting or sleeping in their cabins. Trouble is, no one saw him go. There's only the blood on the deck and rail to show anything. We have to assume he went over the side.'

'Yeah, and injured, too.'

'He didn't have a life jacket either. They found it in his cabin.'

'What about his other stuff?'

'It's all there as far as I can tell, even his dirty washing. His bunk was unmade; probably had a nap before his midnight shift.'

'Watch!'

'What?'

'It's called a "watch" on a ship, not a "shift",' said Pearson.

'Yeah, *whatever*, Captain Sinbad.'

'Don't get cheeky, Constable. Go find the steward. See if you can narrow the time a little.'

Pearson watched as the younger man moved along the deck and disappeared through a hatch.

Sinbad, eh. He smiled, Owens was all right, if a little impertinent at times. Good at his job too.

He entered the wheelhouse and perched on a stool behind the helmsman. It was warmer here, out of the wind. The other two occupants pretended to ignore him, staring instead at the white-flecked sea ahead. He liked it that way.

An accident was the most likely cause of the disappearance, but the Chief Officer was an experienced seaman. Then there was the blood. If it was murder there was no shortage of suspects.

He shook his head again.

It could've been worse.

On this route the ship only needed a crew of eight and, unless there was a conspiracy, four of them had alibis. The others claimed to have been in their cabins but he suspected at least one of them was lying.

He pulled a sheet of paper from his jacket. In the rush to board the *Nakhodka 137* he barely had time to get a list of the crew before they boarded the pilot boat. His stomach was still trying to recover from the three hours of torture as they pursued and finally boarded the tanker.

He consulted the list of names on the page: Captain Irina Khakamada, Seaman Stanisloff Cyrilovic, and Cook Olga Benovic. All women except for the seaman, did it mean anything?

Pearson was getting to know the ship now. He found the stairs and descended to the lower deck. The air smelt of fresh paint and salt: the walls and ceilings uniformly white; the deck covered in polished plastic in the colours of the shipping company.

All around details in polished brass and varnished timber suggested nautical quality. Nothing too good for a crew who spent most of their lives at sea! He walked through a heavy door to the narrow outer deck. The wind struck again and the salt smell of the sea seemed more intense than ever. Only a slight vibration betrayed the rapid progress of the ship. After a few yards he came to a small taped-off section. He knelt and examined the scene again, the drops of blood on the deck already darkened to a sticky black. The smaller drops on the rail almost disappeared against the dark timber.

He tried to picture the scene from the previous night when the ship's First Officer vanished. No moon, little light from the interior of the ship, it would be difficult to see.

He ran his hand along the varnished rail to where the first few drops began. Nothing! He stepped over the patch on the deck and ran his hand from the other side of the blood drops further along the rail, his hand stopped by a slight stickiness. He rubbed his fingers together, stared at them and brought them to his nose. *Something there! Constable Owens could take samples.*

As though by mental command, Owens appeared from behind. 'Between ten and twelve last night, as far as anyone can tell, Sergeant. The cook, Olga Benovic, was the last to see him alive. That was in his cabin at ten when she took him a snack, but his … watch, was not due to begin until midnight. That's when he was missed.'

Pearson pursed his lips and paused, his eyes fixed on the deck. He began to speak, slowly as though to himself.

'He was murdered by someone he knew well. Lured to this spot, hit on the head and thrown overboard.'

Owens eyes widened and his mouth dropped open.

'How can you say that? It's all guesswork, you can't know that!'

Pearson pierced his assistant with narrowed eyes and continued. 'This section of deck is not on the Chief Officer's regular route to the bridge. It's out of sight from the common areas and not likely to be visited late at night.'

'Yeah well, maybe he just wandered here and had some sort of accident.'

'No, I don't think so. The rail is more than a metre high. It would be impossible to accidently fall. Besides, I discovered new evidence, sticky patches on the rail. Something was held there with adhesive tape.'

He looked at the other, but no flash of insight disturbed Owens's bland round face.

'I think he was lured here on some pretext,' he repeated. 'He was shown something stuck to the rail, then as he bent to examine it was hit from behind. Slumped over it was simple to grasp his ankles and flip him all the way. If he hadn't bled so much we would never have found the spot. He would have simply disappeared.'

He turned suddenly to Owens,

"What did they say about him, the victim, Chief Officer Andrei Tarkovsky?"

Owens shook himself from a moment of reverie and pulled a pad from his pocket.

'Seaman Stevenovich and the Steward did not know him before the voyage, but thought he seemed nice enough. Captain Khakamada thought he was a fine young fellow, intelligent and caring, a good Chief Officer. The Second Officer and the Engineer said he was a good seaman and had plenty of personality but appeared to be a bit of a womaniser, if his stories could be trusted. The strangest one was the cook, Olga Benovic. She seemed really broken up about his disappearance. I had trouble getting her statement, but eventually she said much the same as the captain.'

'Have another word with her. She probably knows more than she's telling. Something's not quite right with her story. I'll talk to the captain again.'

He found his way to the captain's cabin and knocked. The door opened immediately and Captain Khakamada invited him in.

She was a short stocky woman in her late thirties, light brown hair in a conservative cut and only a slight suggestion of make-up. She wore her white captain's uniform with quiet dignity.

'Good evening Sergeant. How are your investigations going?' she said, shaking his hand formally. She spoke slowly in a low, husky voice, its Russian accent adding an attractive edge to a tone of authority.

He'd apparently interrupted her at the end of a meal. The smell of boiled cabbage hung in the air and a tray with cup and plates on a small table confirmed his observations. She returned to a chair at the table and gestured for him to sit opposite, replacing a linen serviette on the tray as she did so.

'Good evening, Captain. I'm sure you know my investigations are at the information gathering stage at this point. However, I can tell you Chief Officer Tarkovsky was murdered and his body thrown overboard between 10pm and midnight last night.'

'Murdered you say, there's a murderer on my ship?'

Pearson studied her carefully. The level of fear in her voice and the expression and concern on her face, were almost perfect. 'Why don't we drop this façade, Captain? He was your lover, but you caught him with Olga Benovic, the Cook, no less. It was more than your pride could stand. You lured him on deck, knocked him unconscious and threw him overboard. A crime of passion if you like, but well planned.'

He watched her face for a flicker of surprise or remorse, but her square features remained expressionless. When she spoke it was in the same slow tone as before.

'Ridiculous Sergeant. You have no way to show I knew Chief Officer Tarkovsky beyond our professional relationship. As for killing him, look at me, I'm barely five feet tall. He was almost six feet and stocky too. How could I kill him? Ridiculous!'

'Size is not a problem when the victim is unsuspecting and the killer is skilled, Captain. You know that. I felt the calluses on your hands when we shook, where did you train? Russian navy? Marines, perhaps? It will come out. As for your affair, Miss Benovic will soon confirm she was sleeping with the victim. She may even have known about you."

She jerked to her feet pushing the chair back with a crash and took a half step towards him, her face now a genuine mask of fear and hatred.

'You'd better go, Sergeant. And I advise you not to repeat these stupid accusations. I intend to make a formal complaint to my embassy.'

Pearson backed a few steps, turning as he placed his hand on the door latch. 'If you wish, Captain! But I should point out that we will be out of Australian waters very soon and I suggest you consider whether you prefer an Australian gaol or a Russian firing squad.'

She was silent for a moment, staring into his eyes yet seeing something he couldn't know. She took a few steps forward then collapsed, like a puppet released of its strings; a jumble of cloth and bones. Pearson made no attempt to help her as she looked up with a face now contorted with anguish, her facade of strength and authority destroyed.

'He was supposed to love me. We planned a future together. How could he do that? All for that ...!' Then something in Russian he did not understand.

The pilot boat thumped across the choppy sea at full speed. Pearson decided he hated the irregular, rolling and jerking, though his stomach didn't seem to mind. *Perhaps I'm getting my sea legs.* The police constable from Mackay and the Russian embassy fellow sat with the prisoner between them. Her eyes downcast and her uniform crumpled, she'd not said more than a few words since the night before.

It was impossible to talk or move about on the wild ride, but Constable Owens, his face the colour of bleached coral, stood at the centre of the cabin his eyes fixed on the sea ahead and a bucket by his side. He'd given up his breakfast of bitter tea and herrings to the sea but Pearson was fairly certain he was not looking for his next meal.

And anyway, it was probably not a good time to tell him, it could've been the cook.

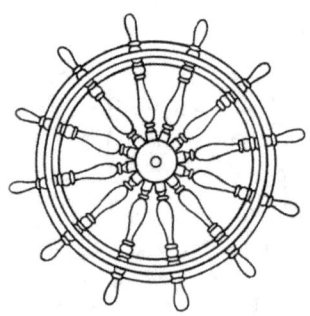

Murder in Spirit

The first I knew of the murder was when the police came to my office the following morning. I was writing up the details of a fidelity case. Since sitting down to write, the rain had stopped, and thin strands of sunlight were stabbing through the overcast. I'd paused, searching for a suitable simile, when the buzzer on my desk announced a visitor at the front of the building. Mrs. Williams would have to wait a little longer to hear about her husband's peccadilloes. Maybe it was a new client.

'Pahla and Company Investigations,' I announced, trying the tone of aloof importance I believed new clients preferred from a larger business.

'Police here, Mr. Pahla. I'm Detective Sergeant Anders. Could we have a word?'

'Police? Yes, of course. Come in.'

I jabbed at the remote release with nervous haste and Anders was at my office door before I could lever my ageing frame around the desk.

I opened the door at his knock.

'Detective Sergeant Anders,' he said smiling faintly and showing me his identification in a battered blue wallet.

'Robert Pahla,' I announced, grasping his extended hand and returning the smile. 'Please come in. Would you like tea or coffee?'

'Neither thanks, where can I put this umbrella?'

'Over there will be fine.'

I waved my hand at the waste paper bin near the door and he placed a dripping blue umbrella next to my somber black model.

We exchanged formal introductions and minor pleasantries while I took his coat and hung it on the hat stand behind my desk. My mind boiled with possibilities but he was clearly not in a hurry to get to the point of his visit.

'Please take a seat,' I said finally.

At my gesture he sat in the old bucket seat I keep for visitors; the one liberated from Vinnie's when I set up the investigation business in the hope it would give the office an established and professional air. He sank gratefully into its black vinyl embrace.

I took the opportunity to observe him carefully.

He was a large man and he wore a grey suit that probably fitted him better ten years earlier, junior rugby league I'd say. He probably hadn't played football since school, now beer and late hours had taken their toll and rounded his body in all the wrong places. His face had a pale podgy look. I was reminded of a potato with glasses and receding hair. I smiled at the image behind what I hoped was my bland business-like face.

He smelt of tobacco and stale beer but he still moved with the grace of an athlete and he kept my now puzzled expression unanswered, his dark eyes never leaving me, until he was seated. He was clearly examining me with the same eye for detail that I was applying to him. What did he see? A little brown man with grey hair, I presumed.

'Do you know Raymond Furfanti?'

'Yes, Raymond ... Ray's head of the Furfanti family. Criminals all of them,' I replied. 'I've never done any work for them. What's this all about?"

He studied me carefully before replying.

'Mr. Furfanti was murdered last night.'

'That's terrible ... though not a loss. How can I help?'

Instead of answering, he reached into an inner pocket and slid a square of paper to me.

'We thought you might recognise this.'

I recoiled from the photograph in shock and recognition.

'Yes, it's my knife, my Kris,' I said slowly. 'Where did you find it?'

'Your knife was in Mr. Furfanti's back.'

I sat back in my executive swivel chair. A thousand questions crowded out articulate speech. I felt my mouth drop open, and closed it with a snap as I sat down heavily, my mind a fog of confusion.

'I don't understand. My Kris was stolen from my home a week ago with a lot of other stuff from my collection. It was my favourite piece and very important to me for personal reasons. I reported it to the police. When can I get it back?'

He ignored my question and continued.

'Yes, I know you reported it. That's how I knew where to come.'

'You can't believe I killed Furfanti. I was here last night working late.' My voice squeaked in rising indignation. 'I didn't even know the man.'

'Take it easy Mr. Pahla,' he smiled. 'We know you didn't do it. In fact, we already have the killer. Do you know a Mr.

Brendon Bailey? He was found with the body but claims he can't remember what happened. We just need more details.'

I was already beginning to like this Sergeant Anders.

'Bailey? Certainly, he was a client for a while. He's the killer? Why are you asking these questions if you already know?' He did not reply and asked a question of his own.

'Would Bailey have known about your collection?'

'Sure, we met at my home once or twice. I showed it to him. He must have realised how valuable it was.' He made some notes in a small notebook before replying.

'The defence counsel will ask about the murder weapon. I need to know as much as possible about everything associated with the case,' he said patiently, 'Tell me about your collection. Was it valuable?'

'Yes, but it's hard to put a price on it. Weapons collectors can pay any price for a good piece. Some of my items could be very valuable, only an auction would tell for sure. Anyway, mine is insured for a couple of million dollars.'

For the first time he appeared genuinely surprised.

'Wow! Millions for some old swords and guns. That's amazing!'

'Not to a collector, mine is the best collection of ancient Javanese weapons in existence. My Kris, Hantu Kebal alone could be worth half a million but I'd never sell it.'

'Why not?'

I looked at him closely as I considered how to begin. Outside the rain had stopped, and a feeble sun was casting weak shadows across the worn carpet.

'Do you know what a Kris is?' I asked.

He admitted he didn't, so I launched into one of my familiar lectures. 'A Kris is a type of dagger common throughout southeast Asia. It sometimes has a wavy blade and is usually richly- decorated. Kris daggers are considered spiritual objects with magical powers. Some older Javanese believe a Kris can transfer these powers to its owner. There are books on the subject if you'd like to know more.' I paused and took a deep breath. Anders did not interrupt and appeared to be genuinely interested in my story.

'Should I go on?' I asked.

'Yes, yes. I'm very interested. It's fascinating. Please go on.'

'My father was a Javanese prince. Yes, I know what you're thinking, I suppose all boys would like to believe their fathers were special, but mine actually was. He married my mother and lived here as an academic; then when I was a baby he returned to Java to support the war of independence against the Dutch. He never returned. I only know about him from my uncles.'

The room dimmed suddenly as a fragment of cloud obscured the sun. "Hantu Kebal" means *Invulnerable Ghost*, it was given to my father by his father. It had … *has* been in the family for centuries. Anyway, as my mother told it, he said to her the night before he left, 'The boy needs his family Kris. It will guide and protect him and those he loves. It will link him to his ancestors and make him invincible in battle. With a hand on his Kris he will know he doesn't stand alone.'

I paused, for a moment, a boy again, running through the house in my Batman suit …

'The Kris has always been part of our family. It hung in our lounge until my eighth birthday.'

I blow out the candles and see my mother taking the Kris from the wall and handing it to me; my sisters and the other kids standing around wide-eyed and silent for a change, as she says to me, 'Your father gave this to you when you were a baby. He said it would protect you. Little good it did him. It's always been yours. Now I want you to take it into your room, put it away, and never talk of it again. You're old enough to look after it, but don't take it

outside. I don't want you running about with it. And …
and …' Tears welled in her eyes and she reached for me
and held me close. Even then, I knew something was
different. My father's image grew in my mind and took
shape. A regal brown warrior wearing a curious black and
green cap, a bandolier of cartridges strung across his chest
and the hilt of my Kris jutting from a white sash above his
sarong. His misty form seemed to be running through a
forest, slightly crouched with one hand carrying a rifle and
the other steadying his *parang* as the scabbard flapped
against his thigh. His face was a hero's face, full of courage
and determination. In my child's eye, he feared neither man
nor spirit.

Anders did not seem surprised by my pause and I began
again. Feeling slightly embarrassed at my unexpected
passion I collected my thoughts and crossed the room to
put on the jug. Neither of us spoke as I made a pot of tea.
Anders accepted a shortbread biscuit then sat back and
asked me to tell him more. I began by describing the other
pieces of my collection in great detail. There was a lot to
tell, but he listened intently and asked a few questions from
time to time. I thought for a while I might've found
another ancient weapons enthusiast. Finally, I could think
of nothing more to say. Most of the morning had gone and
my stomach told me it was close to lunch. I thought
Anders must've been reluctant to ask the questions on his
mind; then, just as I glanced at the clock, he said, 'Tell me
more about your Kris. What are these supernatural powers
it is supposed to possess?'

I could not help smiling at him. 'You're not starting to
believe in this stuff, are you? It's just myth and legend, you
know.'

He did not seem amused, just regarded me intently with
his small dark eyes until I continued.

'Invincibility - and invisibility - mostly! Very much *Harry Potter* stuff. But I suppose if you even half believed it, it might give you courage in battle. Not unlike Excalibur or the Scots with their dirks in British legends, I suppose. If *Invulnerable Ghost* lived up to its name it would be worth a lot more than half a million dollars,' I chuckled.

For a long moment we sat looking at each other. He held a curious blankness on his face. The seconds dragged into minutes. Neither of us wanted to restart the conversation. At last I coughed and was about to say something when he spoke. As he did so, he leant forward and looked intently into my eyes as if anxious to receive my judgement, or at least, understanding.

'We figure they were arguing,' he began, 'probably about the collection. We think Bailey realised its true value, though needed someone like Furfanti to fence it for him. At some point they disagreed, maybe, and Bailey lost his temper and stabbed Furfante in the back using your Kris."

'Then why ...,' I began.

'The curious thing is Furfanti's two thug cousins, who were at the door supposedly guarding him, swear Bailey had left the office five minutes beforehand and had not returned. They had to break down the door when they heard their boss scream.

'We interviewed them very ... forcefully, but both of them swear their boss was alive, working at his desk alone when they last saw him. They swear Bailey did not return past them, but it seems he did. It's as though he was invisible, but that's impossible, isn't it?' He raised his eyebrows as though to excuse himself from his ridiculous question.

'Well you seem to have your man,' I said. A low chuckle that could've been thunder, sounded faintly. Anders did not seem to hear it. I saw my father dimly, smiling by the window, shot through with shafts of sunlight. Still smiling he faded and vanished. I shivered slightly from a sudden chill in the air.

'Why don't we have lunch while we talk some more, Detective Sergeant?' I suggested as I took my coat from the rack near the door.

The vinyl squeaked as he levered his weight from the bucket seat.

'Sure, I could use a drink,' Anders said and we walked into the sunlight.

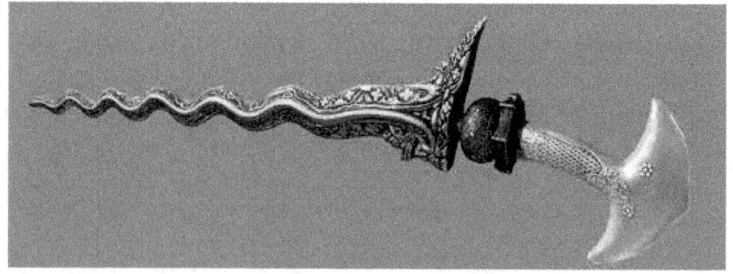

Homecoming

'Mr. Harris?'

'Who's calling?'

'It's Sally from Car Sales, about the demonstration drive. The *Lotus*?' Her voice was young yet she was not disturbed by my abrupt manner.

'Please let Mr. Harris know one of our staff will meet him at 3.00 pm, as arranged, would you?'

We concluded the conversation with the usual insincerities and I returned to my book. I would be outside the church in Artarmon at 3.00. It was a busy public place though not likely to be monitored. And the Federal Police are not known for their intelligence anyway.

I'd been looking forward to a spin in the new *Lotus Sprint 220*. Perhaps I would buy it; a little ostentatious though within the apparent income of a senior airline captain. A brief moment of fantasy, even in the company of a garrulous salesman, would be worth it. One problem with *'ill-gotten gains'* is they are often difficult to spend without raising attention.

I was about to get up when a movement in the corner of my eye gave me a brief start, yet it was only Raffie, the pool guy, passing the window as he gave the pool its weekly brush up. His white shorts and striped blue tee shirt gave him a nautical look, perfect for the harbour backdrop. Under a broad canvas hat his sharp brown face frowned in concentration as he dragged some anonymous piece of equipment along the terrace. I was never sure how much serious work he did. Still, the pool was always spotless and the water sparkling, that was all I wanted. It was rarely used. I kept it for show.

It is important to present the correct image when you want to blend in and the apartment was a part of that. The real estate woman was effusive in pointing out the features of the place when I bought it. *The light aqua tints, its tiled floors, the wonderful view of the Opera House visible under the Bridge, its Mediterranean 'feel'.* She need not have bothered with the pitch, for me it was all about appearances. I saw the real Mediterranean about once a month from exclusive luxury hotels with no star ratings, but I needed to have a home.

I needed to fit in and become part of a community.

It is my habit to walk after breakfast. Others in our block had similar habits so I was not surprised when the lift was already occupied by Betty Philips.

'Good morning, Betty, you're up early,' I said as the doors opened.

'I like to get to the shops before they're crowded, Alan. Do you want me to get you anything?'

'No thanks, I've got everything I need. Thanks anyway.'

Betty is a stalwart of the *Owner's Corporation* managing our unit block. They invited me to join once and it would've been a good way to become part of the community, but my constant travels made it impractical.

'Where are you off to next, Alan?'

'I'm on a break at the moment. After that it'll be the London route for a month.'

'Oh, I love London,' she said. 'Howard and I lived there once. We had to return to Sydney when he became ill ...' She paused and was quiet for a moment. Howard, now long gone, had been something in the Foreign Service and Betty must've matched him in intelligence and poise as they represented us to the British. Beneath her grey hair and frumpy appearance lurked a sharp and imaginative mind. I needed to be extremely careful when I was around her.

The lift doors opened and Betty and I went our separate ways into the bright morning.

A light breeze from the harbour brought the sweet scent of spring as I started my morning walk.

At 10.15am I was in *Giorgio's* at my usual summer table by the garden. The place was crowded, but that suited me. I put down my newspaper and checked the time, then reached for my phone. Before I could get it out of my pocket, it rang with the familiar Rock & Roll tune that I affected.

'You're becoming predictable,' I said.

A light female chuckle, then, 'Only when I want to be; as you should know!'

It was Sandra of course.

'Anything this week?' she asked. She was being indiscreet yet I couldn't say anything openly.

'I'm rostered for a two week break, then its London via Bangkok for a few days.' I hoped she would see the implications.

'Bangkok, yes, I think we can recommend something there. I'll set it up. I'm on US flights via Hawaii for a few weeks, so we won't see much of each other for a while. I'm due out in a few minutes, so I'll see you later.'

'OK, give me a call when you're back.'

I sat back and looked beyond the lawn to the jacarandas framing the harbour. The first patches of colour were appearing in the topmost twigs; soon the trees would be covered with a purple canopy. It was five years since I first met Sandra. Our relationship was complex, a combination of mutual greed, distrust and lust. She was the only one who knew my full story; and without her, the business died. She arranged the shipments and got them onto the flights. As an airhostess, she had her ways. I never enquired how. the process quite unknown to me. My job was to get them through customs and into Sydney, she never questioned my system.

I'd not expected our relationship to develop past the carnal when we first met. Sure, she was beautiful, intelligent and fun to be with, but at that time she was just another conquest.

Giorgio stopped by my table for a few minutes. He was a little flushed from the kitchen, but his dark features were smiling. We know each other well. He was too much of the professional restaurateur to sit and chat for long, but we exchanged a few pleasantries and he reminisced briefly with a boring anecdote about his boyhood in Trieste. I took the opportunity to make a dinner booking. The food was good and I hated cooking for myself.

I was in a good mood when I arrived home later in the evening. Everything was running smoothly and after three years my only problem was how to spend the money without it being noticed. I relaxed, replete with Giorgio's *Barramundi Mediterranean* and a glass of wine, and tried to read more of my book. I was rereading *Kidnapped*, a book I'd read at school. I don't like to think too much about my boyhood and schooldays, though one thing I did enjoy was our English class. I could escape into the classics and imagine myself doing daring things in far-away places. I admired David Balfour's independence and fortitude in the book. How could Stevenson have mirrored my own feelings of loneliness and isolation so closely? I took a sip of my wine, opened the book at the last place and kept reading. David was at his uncle's castle in the Highlands …

It was a one-sided battle, my eyes kept drooping and I needed to read each line twice to follow the meaning.

I stirred with my sister's hand on my chest.

She stood on tiptoe; her thin body half my height.

'Don't go, Alan, you belong here,' she was saying.

Her face ran with dusty tears, she was just sixteen, forever young. 'Mum and Dad can't run things without you; and all your school mates are here.'

'I have to go,' I said, in my teenage voice.

My father shook my hand and my mother cried.

Our words were spent.

I was looking back as the taxi took me away.

I wanted to look forward towards the exciting future but my mother's face captured me, growing smaller and smaller, until it was eclipsed by a small dip in the road.

I woke with a start as Kidnapped slipped from my fingers; I had not had that dream for months and it brought back bitter memories of loss and hurt. I was with them. We were on our way into town to the pictures. My father turned the old ute over the cattle grid and out the farm gateway onto the main road. We all sat together like corpses as the semi-trailer rose over the hill ahead, all blinding lights and blaring horn filling the road. Sudden fury of sound and twisted metal. All gone. My family all gone now but not me, why? How had I offended the universe to deserve this?

'The little packets, be careful who you sell them to, compadre,' said Santos in his Catalonian accent. 'There are many police spies and informants about. This fool of a mayor wants to ruin the tourist trade,' he spat in the general direction of the town hall as I continued to wipe the counter.

'The Brits and Americans like to get their "little packets" from someone who speaks English. Can you get me more?'

Santos eyed the door to the bar nervously now.

'It is too dangerous. I do not have your nerves, but I will make a call for you.'

A few days later the embassy managed to find me. The caller was female, young, and anxious to hang up the telephone as quickly as possible. I remember clearly the curiously foreign Aussie accent over a crackling line from Madrid. I do not blame her for her hasty words of condolence and formal offer of assistance. There was nothing to be done.

I left the bar soon after, it was probably time to leave Seville anyway. Travel became my passion for a while, but it was like wandering through an open zoo. Each country was its own small section but nowhere where you would want to stay, nowhere to belong. School friends wrote to me occasionally, but I never replied. Eventually they stopped writing. In Lucerne, I discovered how easy it is to set up a Swiss bank account. It was just as well, my usual bank account was starting to look a little over-stuffed for a bartender.

In London students and staff at the Polytechnic were quite keen to try my 'little packets.' Life as a student helped to round my vowels and my piggy bank for a couple of years before I felt it wise to move on again.

In Bangkok, I met people who seemed to have found meaning in life. I took a far-from-onerous job with an airline company. Buddha seemed to smile down benignly from every bend of the river and I studied with mounting interest, hoping to join my friends in their peace-of-mind and compassion.

But peace did not come for me.

'Perhaps you need a change of scenery. Would you like to take a package to Chang Mai for us?'

'I would be pleased to, though don't you have cheaper ways to transport things?' I queried.

'This package is rather sensitive and no-one will question a foreigner.'

I was skeptical, yet bored. I took some leave from the airline and headed north. The 'package' turned out to be a heavy crate about the same length as an AK47.

I was generously rewarded.

This seemed a good time to do some pilot training in Sydney; it showed my *dedication to the company* and my *ambition*, so my supervisor said.

I think she was rather jealous.

It was certainly convenient for me.

I left Bangkok within days.

It turned out to be a pivotal point in my life. I met Sandra in pilot training, though it was a couple years later we set up our business. Now she, and a few others, even Giorgio and Betty, are my family. This is where I feel most at home. There is no farm to return to.

Hindsight is a thing of clarity and regret, but no matter how obvious the disaster now appears; no one could've foreseen the coming events. My world was about to shatter yet I went about life like a bird building its nest, unaware of the approaching storm. The first inkling of trouble was on Tuesday after my usual Rotary club meeting, when a couple of cars left the darkened car park in my wake. I convinced myself it was coincidence flavoured with paranoia, and put it out of my mind. I should've been more attentive.

On Wednesday, I noticed Raffie looking sideways at me from time to time as he skimmed fallen leaves from the pool. I checked my wallet and waited for him to ask for a pay rise, but he didn't say anything. It was another clue I somehow missed. That must have been when they bugged my apartment. How disappointed they must've been.

I've always been a good sleeper and Thursday night was no exception. I was asleep when a tremendous crash at the front door woke me. Before my body could react the crashing sounds continued. The door must've finally given to their sledgehammers and I was only partly out of bed when the clatter of boots and loud shouts sounded in the hall. A shadow appeared by my bed and I was pushed back roughly. The dawn light was enough to recognise a shotgun as its huge barrel was thrust into my face. Behind the gun a dim face with a black mask and helmet.

More shouts:

'Clear,' a male voice.

'Clear,' a younger female voice.

"Kitchen clear," a different male voice with a nervous pitch.

"Very good, Sergeant," a calmer male voice near my bed, "search the house."

Still too terrified to talk, I could only stare dumbly as my tormentor brushed my book off a chair and sat down.

"Now Mr. Harris, let's have a little chat." His melodramatic words should've been laughable but I wasn't amused. He was young and of medium height as far as I could tell, with a dark face and a prominent scar at the corner of his mouth. He peered at me intently with vivid blue eyes as he began his questions.

"I'm Detective Inspector Pidoso from the Federal Police narcotics division," he began and showed some sort of card in a leather wallet. My brain was still too confused to focus, but I managed to squeak;

"What do you want? What's going on? Can I get dressed?" I was still in my summer pyjamas.

"We've been watching you for some time," he began, ignoring my question. "We know that you have been bringing drugs into Australia. You are under arrest and will be formally charged later. Your cooperation could assist you in court," he sneered as he finished his little speech, "Now, Just tell us where you keep the drugs?"

"Are you crazy. I don't have anything like that. You only had to knock, I'd have let you in. "

"Let's not play games. We've been watching you and your friends for weeks. We know how your operation works."

"You must have the wrong person. There are no drugs here," I shouted with all honesty and indignation. I could afford to be generous with the truth.

Pidoso tried to confuse me with combinations of questions and threats. He must've thought he was smarter than me. His word games and traps only stopped when a female officer in a baggy black jump suit appeared and gave him a thumbs down sign.

That night in my cell, I couldn't sleep at first; the day's events had seemed so fantastic, so surreal that I could scarcely believe them. My system had been perfect, nothing could go wrong, yet it had. The narrow concrete walls, dim light and smell of urine forced me to realise that my world had changed. Exhausted by the day's events, I closed my eyes. I woke to the screech of the iron hatch as they pushed my breakfast tray through the door. My new life had begun.

The first to visit was my solicitor, Geoff Roberts. His familiar face was a relief from the four pastel walls when he appeared later that morning.

'Alan, I am sure that this is all a terrible mistake. Don't worry, we'll soon have you out of here.'

Geoff had done some conveyancing for me and we'd played cards at Giorgio's a few times. I know him to be shrewd and intelligent. Yet sometimes even the brightest of people can miss the obvious. It was almost amusing to watch his eyes widen in surprise at my answers to his questions but he settled down when he realised the changed nature of our connection. After an hour or so, he brightened and I think he began to enjoy the change from our mundane suburban relationship. He now worked for a real criminal doing exciting things; the money was hardly a consideration.

Remarkably, Giorgio was my next visitor. Perhaps he secretly admired me; his ancestors had been smugglers, he had once confided, but I think he drew the line at drugs. He passed me a copy of the local paper. There I was, in my captain's uniform, on the front page in the smiling pose of an airline poster boy. It was one of my best pictures. They used the same photo in the Sydney Morning Herald but on the second page. Infamy is just the flip side to fame after all and both are short lived.

I was a standout super villain for a few days.

On Saturday I was no longer news and my story had slipped to a few column-inches on the inside pages of the *Daily Telegraph*.

Where I'd once hidden in blessed obscurity, I now stood revealed, as a drug smuggler, a pariah.

The trial was stressful. I sat all day on a hard bench in the dock trying to look innocent and concerned as my legal counsel battled with the other side over each legal point.

The seat was hard but hearing the details of my early life paraded made it worse. I was not alone. Jim Blair shared the dock with me. Orange prison garb is not flattering and we must've appeared a particularly strange couple. Jim looks more like an overweight jockey than an airport security officer, whereas I'm more the beanstalk figure.

I had every reason to be morose and could hardly bear to look at Jim. He was the cause of my problems; the weak link I ignored. They knew drugs were coming in and a background check of airport personnel threw up a few suspects. Jim had a minor criminal record as a teenager; we thought it was too trivial to worry about. How wrong we were, he was quickly identified and they set up surveillance on him.

The details were revealed at the trial. After months of covert observation, one sharp-eyed young officer noted that Jim sometimes had trouble with eyestrain. The x-ray security station takes concentration; it is hard on the eyes. On occasions, Jim would ask someone to relieve him for a few minutes. It only took a second or two. He'd stand, stretch and wait for his replacement to take over the x-ray station. At that moment, the contents of the now transparent bag would be displayed in the machine in brilliant colour, but there were no eyes to see it.

Was it coincidence that those occasions often happened when flight crew were passing through security? Not any flight crew, one senior captain in particular, me.

They had us both.

After Giorgio left, Detective Pidoso appeared again. He seemed short and gnome-like flanked by two large prison officers, yet I wasn't feeling amused as they led me to an interrogation room. All those TV dramas I'd watched had prepared me for this: the classic two-way mirror wall, a side table with recording equipment and a sturdy wooden table. Disturbingly, there were also several rings let into the polished concrete floor. I presumed these were for securing the shackles of dangerous prisoners.

I was pushed into a heavy steel chair.

It was excruciatingly uncomfortable.

Pidoso sat opposite in a wooden chair, though it did not look any more comfortable than mine.

The whole atmosphere made me extremely nervous, doubtlessly as intended.

One prison officer left the room but the other stood poker-faced behind me near the door. This would become our routine for the next few months while I was in remand, and later in a nearly-identical room at my prison.

The first thing Pidoso wanted to know was where to find Sandra. I told him, truthfully, I had no idea; that we'd worked independently and not once confided those sorts of details with each other.

Sandra had disappeared, presumably pre-warned, somewhere in the US, it was thought. I knew blonde was not her natural colour so I suppose she just cut and dyed her hair, changed eye colour with contact lenses and faded into the crowd. With those changes, even I could pass her in the street and not recognise her. With her drug contacts, she would have no trouble finding false documents. Maybe she was now part of some obscure community somewhere. She spoke five languages and had years to prepare her background.

Prison life is just as I imagined it: dull, boring and monotonous. In remand, I began to learn the realities. The routine never varied: sleep, food, visitors, interrogation, food, interrogation again, one hour exercise yard, food, sleep – press 'repeat.'

It was a relief when the trial was over and I was moved to Silverwater Prison to begin my sentence.

I awoke with a jerk, sitting upright and almost hitting my head on the bunk above. The incessant clamour of the bell was as melodious as two schoolboys with sticks and a tin can.

Somehow, Bruce on the bunk above managed to sleep through it, even continuing the snoring to which I was yet to become accustomed. I shook him awake.

Big Bruce is my cellmate and we are close. Not in the Sandra type of closeness, you understand, Bruce is a married man with a wife and three children in Bankstown, but close none-the less. He's my 'minder'. He knows everything about prison life and nobody bothers me now. He was most appreciative when I arranged for Geoff Roberts to get some money to his family.

At some remote command the cell door clicked and swung open. Bruce can move fast when he wants to and he was already dressed and beside me as we waited for roll call. I've never been a 'morning person' so I was barely thinking as officer *Piggy* Porter approached with his clipboard. He was followed closely by *Darkie* Daoud who fondled his baton as though itching for any excuse to use it. They all had nicknames, though we could not use them openly.

'Harris?' he shouted. I was standing right in front of him.

'Present, Sir,' I shouted, not making eye contact.

He continued talking without moving his lips or taking his eyes from his clipboard. It was a strange sound.

'Any problems, Arty?' I could barely hear him, but I liked his greeting. It had only taken a few days for "Art Class" to become "Arty".

'None I can't handle, Mr. Porter. How'd your wife like the show?'

'Wonderful. She thought opera was crap, now she can't stop talking about it. Thanks'.

He made a note of some kind on his clipboard then swung to Bruce, his voice returning to its natural nasal shout, and confirmed that Bruce was also present. Then, with Darkie in tow, he pointed his stomach at the next cell and the caravan moved on.

Left to our own devices Bruce and I trooped down to the canteen for breakfast.

My first view of the morning's offering made my stomach heave in disgust. I think it might have started as scrambled eggs with tomato and mashed potato, but I cannot be sure. It was a grey mush, relieved in places with mysterious black and red specks. The only clue to its origin was a yellow thumbprint and scrap of eggshell on the edge. As I was pondering this, the tray was quietly taken from my hands and replaced by another. This one had two unmistakable fried eggs and a strip of crispy bacon with two tomato halves on a bed of mashed potato. The tomatoes still had that soft collapsed look from the griller.

'Are we paying them enough, Bruce?' I asked.

'I'll pass the word to sharpen up, Alan. It won't happen again.'

'OK, but don't be too heavy, we all need a second chance.' It pays to spread your largesse, and money, in prison.

Bruce gathered the plastic cutlery and we sat at a corner table with our trays. Bruce knew better than to talk before I started on my first cup of tea, so we sat without a word.

I'd just pushed my tray away when Spider Smith approached and sat down quickly. His grey prison overalls looked a size too big on his long arms and skinny frame.

An old prison hand and part magician, there doesn't seem to be anything he can't get.

'How's the mattress?' were his first words.

'Good morning to you too, Spider,' I said with as much sarcasm as I could muster. 'The mattress is much better. Where'd you get it?'

'Don't ask, I'll send you the bill.'

He was only half joking.

I knew I had to pay for it in some way.

'I wanted to discuss the homework topic you gave the arts class.'

Spider was one of my best students.

'What would you like to know?'

'I don't understand this business about Buddhist styles,' he continued, his voice reflecting his confusion.

'Asian art is often based on religious themes, just like ours. There are several main branches of Buddhism and each is represented differently in their art,' I said 'I'll say more about it in the class.'

He pushed his chair back noisily and looked at Bruce. They both left for the gym talking animatedly about how they would destroy each other at the table tennis table. I don't play table tennis, so I was left for a few minutes in solitary contemplation.

As it often did, my mind went back to the old farmhouse. I could see it clearly; the wide verandas and low green roof. The driveway and horse yard. The little garden at the back where my mother grew carrots and cauliflower for our dinner table. We kept chooks there too. It had been my home. Yes, home, a funny word, really. Once, long ago, I sat with a girl drinking gluhwein and tried to explain. 'A house is not a home,' I said pompously. She understood, she said, she'd lost her house, home and family in the shelling of Sarajevo. I felt ashamed and embarrassed at my own inadequate story. Many people carry scars that do not show. Mine are no worse than many

They are my family now, Bruce, Spider and others; even Piggy and Darky in their way. We each have a story to tell. Some are bloody and full of passion; some are pitiful tales of depravity. Mine is none of these, I made my own decisions and fate drew me here, away from loneliness and towards acceptance and inclusion. I would have preferred the soft life, but prison has its own society and I fit in rather well. My story is adventurous and exciting compared to many. I am respected here; perhaps I should try writing a book. I have plenty of time for it. Only eighteen years and four months until my release, my counselor says.

Release?

Where will I belong then?

A Curious Incident

'**Let** me introduce myself. My name is Leonard Fyfe-Atkins and I'm an actor. Perhaps you've seen me. *Mrs. Wilson's Dilemma? Wollongong Manor?* No? Well, they didn't run for long. Mrs. Wilson was one of my best. I was the brother ...'

The speaker was a tall man in a blue suit slightly too big for him. He smiled with perfect teeth as he reached across the table and offered a thin hand, his grip weak and perfunctory.

'Simon Buttons, writer,' I said.

His hair appeared greased and lay flat in a style I'd not seen for years; and his hollow, slightly-pockmarked cheeks lay in sharp contrast to his prominent ears. I'd seen him earlier as we circulated with our drinks and was to hear a lot more about him as the lunch progressed.

We finished our meal and were saved from more of the actor's theatrical anecdotes when the presentation began. To be honest, I was not very interested in *Native Tribes of the Oronoco* but the pictures were good so I took some desultory notes. Eventually it was over and we were released into a warm afternoon sun to continue our daily rounds. I turned from the club door to walk to the ferry.

'Hello there, going in my direction?' The question emanating from the now-familiar pockmarked face was rhetorical, so I smiled agreement.

That's how it came about that we walked together towards the Quay. We must've appeared an odd couple: a tall gent in the ill-fitting suit and slicked hair; and a short, overweight (I must admit) jeans-and-runners-clad bloke, half jogging to catch up. Still, I'd managed to find a reasonably clean denim jacket for the lunch and my hair was washed and tied in a neat ponytail.

An author of travel books should look the part.

The long strides of my companion quickly ate up the distance to the Quay. I assumed he was hurrying to catch his ferry. To where, I didn't have breath to ask!

It was a surprise when he slowed as we approached a busker on the concourse: a small man wearing high boots, a jacket covered in stars, and a ridiculous tall hat I suppose - he imagined - made him seem more like a magician. He appeared to be performing conjuring tricks for the few elderly tourists who lingered between ferries. I would've continued walking but Fyfe-Atkins seemed attracted to the scene and I didn't want to make a fussy good-bye. I should've been more assertive, because as the busker continued his act, it became apparent my companion was also an expert on street performance, and took every opportunity to advise the magician on how better to present his tricks.

The little man took the advice with stoic forbearance and an occasional thin smile and, as he continued his repertoire, the crowd grew. At last he reached a climax, producing a large silver hoop and calling for a volunteer.

He chose a young woman in a colourful floral dress at the front of the crowd. A little too overdressed for a warm afternoon, I thought. The magician put the hoop on the pavement and asked the girl to step into it. She did so, giggling, and as the little man lifted the silver hoop, a black curtain with silver stars fell from it cutting off our view. He raised the assembly with both hands while uttering loud incantations, until it was above the girl's head then with a shout, whisked the curtain away. To our collective astonishment, the girl stood as before, except that now she wore a slim sheath of blue silk, high heels and pearls about her neck.

It was an impressive trick, but not enough for Fyfe-Atkins. His shouted derision was appalling. Finally, the busker announced he'd one more trick to perform; one he'd not done for many years it was so dangerous. 'I will make a man disappear.'

The curtain seemed to retract into the hoop as he laid it out as before. This time when he called for volunteers there were no takers. Even my companion was curiously silent, until the little man turned to him. 'What about you, sir? Surely you'd like to see my magic from the other side. Or do you think it too dangerous?'

So goaded, Fyfe-Atkins stepped into the ring. The curtain was slowly raised as before this time to a greater height. Exertion showed on the little man's face as be began his routine, but I had the impression that the incantations were not the gibberish of the earlier performance, but rather real words from a strange language. The magician's voice reached a high pitch and he shook the hoop longer than before. I half expected Fyfe-Atkins to burst out from behind the curtain in exasperation, denouncing the charlatan, and spoiling the act.

At last, his brow dripping with sweat the little man gave a final cry, snatched the silver hoop aside and the curtain with it.

Stunned silence fell on the crowd.

Fyfe-Atkins had disappeared.

The crowd erupted in applause and high-pitched cries of delight. The ridiculous hat was quickly passed around as the crowd lingered, perhaps waiting as I was, for the usual miraculous re-appearance. As it became clear that this was not going to happen, the audience slowly dispersed. I watched puzzled as the little man, still wearing the silly hat, scuttled around gathering up his magic paraphernalia and loading it onto a trolley. The girl in the floral dress, now in black jeans and tee shirt, reappeared and soon the two of them disappeared into the crowd. I waited a few minutes longer but eventually concluded that Fyfe-Atkins, the actor, had relished his theatrical exit and was already boarding his ferry.

I confess I was rather relieved as I turned and caught my own ferry home.

I never saw Fyfe-Atkins or the busker again.

Reminiscence

Iwan Susanto pushed up his mask and straightened. The rumble of the lathe died as he killed it with a sharp touch. *A cup of coffee would be good,* he thought, but smoko was long past. The coffee at work was not to his taste anyway, not like the *Kopi Tubruk* his wife made; not like his mother's.

Sometimes he wondered about that too; perhaps things were not quite as he remembered them.

He stretched to clear his head. What was it they said in English?

'Farther fields are greener', or was it *'further fields ....'* Something like that, though he quite understood what it meant.

He was not unhappy. A loving wife and family, friends at the Mosque, a house with food on the table. His workmates treated him with respect and were friendly in their own boisterous way. He drew a vernier calliper from the pocket of his overalls and applied it to the metal in the lathe. *Mrs Lawson's son, James was doing well with his Indonesian lessons too.* Iwan liked that, he marvelled at the acuity of young minds, and the lessons he gave helped him connect with his neighbours. They were good people.

He returned the calliper to his pocket, sighed, and released the product from the grip of the machine. A last critical inspection and he placed it with its brothers in a neat row on the bench, another part for another nameless device.

He'd done six. One more before he finished would be about right. Turning he picked a rough casting from the bin. The lathe rumbled again and strips of shining metal spun from its sharp tool like skin from an orange.

He adjusted a stream of coolant and the familiar smell of oil and heated metal came to him.

An automatic lathe would be good, he could even set up this old one to do most of the the work, but what would he do then? Stand back and watch? He agreed with the boss, the small number was not worth the effort. From the office a shrill tone sounded. Iwan straightened again and the sound of the lathe died, lifeless but not dead ... waiting.

He pushed through the crowd. At the centre of the carriage, where taller people did not seem to press as hard, he settled for the journey.

White cords hung from his ears behind a blank face as music carried him to his mothers village.

It was durian season and the putrid smell of the fruit wafted to him from the forest across the paddy. His mother would not let him bring it into the house, but later when the sun was low, she would make coffee and the family would sit near the old Dutch well and enjoy the fruit with small cakes and talk.

He looked up as the train slowed: *Ashfield.*

Iwan picked up his bag and followed a large woman to the door, the sound of gamelan filled his ears and the scent of durian drowned his senses.

Something for Mother

The track home was long and dusty, but Stevie didn't mind. He had survived for eight summers and was well adjusted to the conditions. He never left home without water, and was careful not to exert himself too much in the heat. Not that he usually thought in those terms: that was his mother's thinking.

For Stevie every day was new and exciting. This was his world and he wanted to explore it. He hefted his pack with its treasured package, moving the thin strap where it cut his neck. It was heavier than he had expected but he'd manage.

He licked his parched lips and drew a shallow breath of the dry air as he adjusted his wide straw hat against the blazing sun. Perhaps there would be some water in the airstill by the time he reached the house; if his mother hadn't put it aside for the baby.

Another curiosity!

A small wriggling thing with brown hair and blue eyes, like his!

Her skin was a shade darker; and many of the women who dropped by the house commented on that; though some admitted they'd never seen another baby. They were becoming rarer. Perhaps they were becoming darker too. A miracle, his mother said. Stevie did not know about that, it was just another wonder in a life of wonders.

He glanced towards the horizon where the sun's bright disk had risen above the hills to dominate the east. Birds! Why were there no birds? His mother had shown him one in a book once. The last one hadn't been seen in his lifetime, she said.

Animals, too!

He'd seen a dead rabbit once. His father said some still lived in their deep cool burrows surviving on remnants of roots. Perhaps they didn't need as much water as birds. His father had skinned the rabbit and his mother cooked it with a little rice from the garden room, but Stevie decided he didn't like meat.

He took another grip on his pack and quickened his step. The rough ground and sharp gravel from the old road did not trouble his bare feet. He needed to be home for mid-morning closedown. He didn't want his parents worried.

He could see the house now, a low grey mound in the waste of dead sticks and blown sand. On one side, the dry wind had stripped the desiccated cover from the yellow clay beneath giving the mound a lop-sided bald appearance, easily recognisable from the scattering of similar mounds in the valley.

At his knock, the thick door swung open a crack and a draft of cool air welcomed him. His mother's concerned face appeared.

'Come in quickly, Stevie. I was worried.'

'Sorry, mum.'

'You went to those caves again, didn't you?'

Stevie thought it better not to answer.

'I worry when you go there, Stevie. Those caves are deep and dangerous. You could get lost and we'd never find you.'

'I know, but there's always something interesting,' he protested.

He knew she wasn't really angry, just concerned for him.

'There's a little water in the still. Get yourself a drink, go to your room and start on your reading. I'll be there in a minute.' She turned towards the kitchen.

"Mum." She turned back at his curious tone.

"I've got a present for you, I ….". He reached into his pack and his grubby fingers fumbled at the wrappings of the package. One of her precious glass jars was revealed. Words of rebuke died in her throat as she saw what it contained. Bright golden fluffy orbs clung to long leaves of impossible green. She had never seen anything so beautiful.

"Its wattle, my god, it is wattle!" she cried.

"I found it near the entrance to a really big cave. Something growing. Do you like it?"

Stevie wondered about the water on her cheek, and then she pulled him close.

Billy and the Tiger

Billy shifted uncomfortably on the polished wooden bench. A burst of childish laughter came dully from the far end of the corridor, echoing up the concrete stairs and past the ranks of silent classroom doors.

His heart beat faster than the raindrops dripping into his dank Roman cell.

He was about to die and the small room felt hot and stuffy. For the thousandth time he glanced at the frosted glass door and the words,

HEAD OF SCHOOL

The elegant gold lettering gave no clues to his fate.

Just as he looked away, the door burst open. A dark head thrust through and a sharp voice called flatly, 'Billy Galloway!'

He jumped, startled.

The rusted gate creaked open and he shuffled into the sunlit arena, a naked gladiator about to face his worst fear.

'This can't go on, Billy. Miss Stevens says you've been telling tales again, this time about her. What do you have to say?'

'Gee sir, I thought it was true. It could have been,' mumbled Billy regarding the scuffed toes of his dusty shoes more closely.

The sun beat down; something moved on the other side of the arena. A low growl ... almost a purr!

'No it could not, Billy! And that's hardly the point. Miss Stevens says you made it all up. It was a lie, Billy!'

Billy thought it wise not to answer.

If he could just keep quiet enough the tiger might lose interest in the helpless Christian.

He may yet escape to fight another day.

'Billy, do you know the difference between "fantasy" and "reality"?'

The sudden softening of the Principal's voice took Billy by surprise. He looked up startled.

The tiger looked at him intently, it was not smiling.

'Yes sir, "fantasy is stuff you imagine, like in the comics or a dream, reality is like on the news, Mum says.'

'Yes. One actually happened, and the other one is made up, or imagined, Billy. This story you've been telling about Miss Stevens,; its fantasy isn't it? It's not true?'

The tiger was smiling now, trying to soothe Billy before taking him off guard.

'I thought it was, sir, until you explained it to me. I thought I saw what I saw, but maybe I imagined it.'

A tiny morsel for the tiger, perhaps he could tame it after all.

'It's not nice to tell stories about the teachers, Billy. Don't you like Miss Stevens? Most of the children like her. She's young, tall and athletic. She has a beautiful wide smile, a wonderful sense of humour and ... '

The tiger halted its stealthy approach with one paw held in the air. Was this a sudden lapse in its concentration? Could Billy be mistaken?

Perhaps his strategy was working.

'Miss Stevens is very nice, sir. I didn't mean to upset her. I thought she'd think my story was interesting.' He bowed his head in submission.

'What do you mean? What did you say to her?'

'I just told her what I saw on my way to swimming training on Sunday morning,' said Billy, pausing.

'A-n-d?'

The word came stretched, loaded with implications Billy couldn't fathom.

'I thought I saw a man coming out of her house, barefoot and carrying his shoes. She was at the door in a dressing gown like my mum's. I've never seen her like that before … but it must've been my imagination.'

Silence.

The tiger crouched, its head in its paws.

Billy could hear his own heavy breathing.

He would polish his shoes when he got home.

'Err, this man you imagined, did he look like anyone you know, Billy?'

'Well, it was very early. A bit dark. I don't know why, but it looked a bit like you, sir.'

"That's ridiculous Billy. How could you imagine the man was me?"

"Oh, It must have been a dream sir. It can't have been real, could it?"

The tiger had vanished.

97

Adrift

The wave crested and Graham braced for the expected plunge as the swell reached its peak, yet the expected pitching fall into the trough did not come. The sea was flatter. Had he been asleep? He tried to look around. Was there a slight lessening of the gloom at one point? Perhaps it was dawn at last, a chance of survival if they could hang on a little longer.

With rising dread he used some of his dwindling strength to twist his body and reach for the still form lashed to the floating scrap of foam to which he clung. It was long seconds before his numb fingers could be certain. Yes, the boy was still alive; but for how much longer? There was barely room for the thin figure, none for him, as he hung to its edge, his weight threatening to capsize it at any moment.. The make-shift raft had once been a hatch-top on the boat; now they clung to it for life.

He slumped back into the water.

His mind drifted vaguely between fugue and reality; was this what it was like to die, like falling asleep leaving Kate alone to mourn? He felt guilty about that; with all his promises. What was it between a man and a woman; a wonderfully confusing soup of lust and love. There was no such confusion or ambiguity with the love of a child. A child was love unconditional. A love not always expressed or appreciated but love none the less.

The boy had grown so much in the past year, and was strong for his age, but he was no match for the overwhelming power of the sea, if they were not rescued soon he would die without waking.

Perhaps that was best.

Graham had always done what he thought best for the boy, though his mother had doubts.

'He's so young, Graham. Are you sure?'

'He'll be alright, Kate,' he reassured her. 'He's a strong boy, he knows the boat and he has to learn sometime. He keeps begging me to go; it's only a matter of time.'

In the end she'd relented; acknowledging her son's inevitable independence but hating the separation.

Graham loved his son too but perhaps he did not show it enough, he admitted to himself. If they survived he would change that. His thoughts turned to his own childhood, even after many years he could still remember the smell of fish and tobacco, and the whiskers that scratched his cheek when his father took him in his arms.

The sky had definitely lightened. He could see the crest of the next wave and a faint glow in one part of the sky. The abating wind no longer flung spray and foam from crest to crest across the grey water. A rhythmic rise and fall had replaced the perilous falls that threatened to overturn the crude raft. The sudden storm that had shattered his fisherman's dreams appeared to be passing.

He tried to wriggle the fingers of his left hand that was thrust through the rope handle of the hatch cover, noting idly how curious it was that he felt no pain from the raw skin. He could still move his fingers he decided; he could let go if the time came. The struggles that threatened to capsize the raft were now past. For now, it was his only lifeline and his only way to stay close to the boy.

It appeared suddenly lighter. Had he been asleep again?

The raft and its precious cargo seemed to be in order. At the next crest he looked desperately about.

Nothing.

In the east fingers of light thrust their way through shredded clouds. In the west; was that a brief glitter of wings highlighted by the gloom, or just more spray and foam? He slumped in despair, all strength gone.

It was just a matter of time.

What would happen to the boy then?

He felt something brush his leg and was instantly alert. *Probably just his trousers against his calf.* A needless alarm, it was difficult to tell in his numb state. With effort he struggled to turn, to check the boy with his free hand, then slumped into the sea again.

Another touch on his foot brought him awake.

How long had he slept?

Sunlight shafted through long hills of water rising from smooth valleys, but the sky was clear. A loud roaring filled his ears as he saw the cause of his panic outlined in the glass green swell. A shark, - a large one - it would not be long now.

The roaring noise increased and a great wind flattened the sea causing smaller ripples that fled quickly away in all directions. The gleaming shape of a helicopter came into sudden view and hovered as the sound beat on them like a fist; a figure in yellow hung waving from a thin rope.

He seemed close enough to touch.

But the shark was closer.

It would win the race.

Graham could visualised its approach with terrible clarity. It would come in quickly, turning on its side and opening its jaws at the last moment as it took the bait.

The figure in yellow was closer but he would be too late. Yet the boy might survive if the raft remained intact. With a defiant croak Graham wrenched his crippled hand free as the shark turned. He had time to see its open jaws and white underbelly as he let himself slip into the quiet depths.

Alfred's Tango

Alfred Jones looked up from his newspaper across the cobbled plaza. The brief autumn thunderstorm had blown the square clear of pedestrians leaving shiny puddles among the scattered tables and sodden cafe awnings. Near the ancient entry gate, an excited child stomped merrily through the water, delighting in the utility of her bright new red gum boots and matching raincoat. It was the only movement to be seen.

Alfred Jones considered his options. He was by nature a cautious man and considered the exercise of logic and thought a game of life. Now, with time on his hands, he would consider all the possibilities before choosing that which best suited his situation. Frowning, he returned to his paper.

Alfred Jones needed money. His mother's small stipend was disappearing fast despite his frugal lifestyle, and he was faced with the real possibility of having to find a job. *An impossibility of course,* he told himself, hoping that the firm threat would spur his subconscious to a more realistic

102

solution. He had never worked in his young life and his observations of other people and their daily rounds did not cause him the slightest envy.

But what to do?

His desultory scan of the financial pages of the paper - that he did not understand - and the news section that was of little use, offered no solution. Alfred Jones did not follow football and did not care which side of the cricket bat was used to strike the ball. Tennis was a mystery. He frowned and flicked to the social pages. It was interesting to note the activities of the wealthy and famous but he did not consider himself a member of their milieu. He arrived at last at the entertainment pages. There were few current films that Alfred Jones had not seen, but he noted one that was showing near the beach and decided to attend the afternoon session.

Now, fully satisfied with his morning's effort, he set out for the Grand Park Hotel. In a few minutes he was climbing the few steps to the impressive mahogany and brass doors. Appearances, he understood appearances. The hotel was neither good nor bad, neither big nor small, neither luxurious nor spartan. It suited his current financial condition without too much discomfort and he was content.

He rang the small bell on the concierge desk and waited.

'Hello Mr. Jones. You're back early today.' The speaker was a dapper little man wearing a purple sports jacket with the hotels crest on the pocket.

'Just dropped in for my coat, Silvio. Are there any messages?'

' 'fraid not, Mr. Jones. Expecting anything urgent?'

'No, not really, but you never know what might turn up. Thanks anyway.' Alfred Jones turned from the desk,

'Ah, excuse me for asking Mr. Jones. But, well this is a little personal, I'm sorry ..But ... can you dance?'

'Why Silvio, I didn't think you cared,' said Alfred Jones smiling, as he turned back to the puzzled manager.

'No, its just that …, well, I met someone and I need to tango by Tuesday,' gushed Silvio in a whisper, clearly not understanding Alfred Jones's clever joke.

'Well as a matter of fact, I dance very well if I may say so myself. Mummy insisted that I learn all of the … . Doesn't matter, yes I can tango. Why do you ask?'

'As I said, I need to learn to tango. Can you teach me?'

'Oh really, Silvio. I'm not a dance teacher. You need a professional. I'm sure there are plenty in the phone book."

'You don't understand, Mr. Jones; no one must know. My reputation would be destroyed. Everyone around here knows that I can do anything. If it came out that I couldn't dance … well, I would be a laughing stuck.'

'That's "stock", Silvio,' said Alfred Jones. 'But I know what you mean' His own assessment of the I can fix anything concierge had taken a sudden dive.

'Er, I'll make it worth your while.'

'Eh? What do you mean?'

'I'll pay you to teach me. Say, $80 dollars. What do you say?'

This was a new experience for Alfred Jones.

No one had offered him money before. He had no idea what one should say or how one should behave. Still, he did need money.

'All right, let's make it $100,' said Silvio, completely misinterpreting Alfred Jones's hesitation, 'I have to know the tango …… .'

'100 is not much money, Silvio … .'

'What, $100 per hour not much! It's more than I earn in a day. If you don't want the job, just say so, Mr. Jones.'

'Very well, I'll do it,' Alfred Jones heard himself say. $100 each hour, he had never heard of such a thing. Though he was the first to admit that he was not experienced in this area. Perhaps it was a normal fee for dance teachers.

Anyway, it was not work, he was a good dancer. It would be a distraction, a game, entertainment.

He began to warm to the idea.

'When would you like to start?'

Much in life is unpredictable and not all of that is bad. In the next few days Alfred Jones found a new interest called 'work'. Not that he would describe it as such; it was too enjoyable to be 'actual' work. Silvio's assignation with the tango dancer apparently went well, though he said very little. He was now Alfred Jones's biggest fan, and it was not long before he was recommended to others. After all, a concierge of his standing knows everything and everyone, does he not?

At first Alfred Jones resisted, but then he found that he was meeting interesting people, being paid and enjoying it. At idle times he wondered how long this had been going on.

Mother's cheque kept arriving regularly.

It often went unbanked for days!

Fussy

Leon would never have described himself as proud; he would've said he was particular or "fussy". He was fussy about his appearance; his shoes were always shining, his trousers pressed and his jacket brushed. He always combed his hair just so, and trimmed his beard carefully. Mr. Wilson said he was the most meticulous cleaner they'd ever had in the building and that was why he was so valuable to the tenants.

He liked the word "meticulous".

He guessed it meant something like fussy.

And he always tried to be friendly to everyone - even those he didn't particularly like: like Mr. Snipe of *Snipe, Snedly and Thatchpole*.

He put the thoughts from his mind. He felt ashamed of what he was about to do, but he had to put his life back in order. He couldn't sleep. He'd lost his appetite. It wasn't right; it couldn't go on like this. It was shameful ... and untidy. He was fussy about his life and he didn't like it when someone messed it up. He reached into his pocket and brought out a $1 coin. This should just be enough he decided, as he inserted it in the slot and selected the number. He knew exactly what to do; he'd thought it out last night and looked up the number in the phone book. He'd have to be careful about what he said, but he'd practised that too.

When the phone was answered, he asked for an extension and waited. A rough male voice said, 'Yes?'

'I'd like to report a crime,' said Leon.

'What's yer name?' asked the voice.

'That doesn't matter,' said Leon softly. He'd seen someone do this on the TV. He knew they would argue, but eventually they would listen to him. Finally, The Voice said impatiently, 'OK, OK what's the crime?'

'I'm a spy,' said Leon. There was no reply so he continued, 'I collect paper from Mr. Edward's office at number 105 and give it to Mr. Snipe of *Snipe, Snedly and Thatchpole*'.

There was a pause; then 'What?'

Leon patiently repeated his story; this might take more than $1 he thought.

'I empty the waste paper baskets in Mr. Edwards's office and give the papers to Mr. Snipe when no one is looking,' said Leon in a whisper.

'Why do you do that?' said The Voice, sounding resigned but a little more interested.

Leon hadn't thought about this part so he was a little unsure. 'I ... I ... Last Christmas Mr. Snipe gave me $100. I thought it was because he liked the work I do, but then last month he asked me to get the waste paper. Of course, I told him I couldn't. He said he'd tell the taxation department about the $100 if I didn't do as he asked,' blurted Leon in one long breath.

'Tell me more about this Mr. Snipe and Mr. ah ... Edwards. What does Mr. Snipe do with the papers?' said The Voice.

'Oh, Mr. Snipe, I think he's a solicitor, I don't know what he does with the papers. Mr. Edwards,? He's Eddy Edwards. Y' know? He's in politics, Minister for Roads, or something,' said Leon.

There was a pause.

'My name's Rogers, and I'd like you to come to my office and tell me some more about this ... hello ... hello!'

Leon had already hung up.

The next week, when the black cars pulled up and the men in dark suits and sunglasses ran up the stairs to Mr. Snipe's office, one of them paused for a second and looked at Leon carefully.

Leon tried to look invisible.

He felt no sense of pride or shame in what he'd done.

It was just a matter of order-being-restored; he was being 'meticulous'.

He adjusted his overalls and picked up his broom.

He would need to be sure to clean Mr. Snipe's office for the next tenants.

A Win for Billy

The pen tasted of plastic and stale spit. Billy liked pencils a lot better: the wood fibres; the smell; the way your teeth left little holes in the paint; but Brother Michael would not let them use pencil. He rested his elbows on the desk and gazed out the window. The feeble sun lit the yard below with weak indifference. He screwed his face, picked up the pen, and began to write:

The sheriff drew his six-gun and shot the gool through the right eye, black blood oozed.

He would have to think carefully about this.

He wanted to get a **C**, not to fail completely. It took a lot more effort, he decided with a sigh.

There was no way he wanted an **A** like last year. Sean and Terry still teased him about it.

This year he would win by losing.

He smiled at the idea.

They would be outside playing by now, Sean and Terry. He thought about joining them in the park opposite the house; perhaps later, if his mother allowed.

He applied the biro, carefully writing, *g-o-o-l*. His composition was already pretty bad. Brother Michael wouldn't like the spelling mistakes; he would like the spirits and demons even less. He liked Christian things, the power and ultimate success of the Church.

Billy hoped he wouldn't like this story.

The smell of baking scones wafted from the kitchen below. Billy smiled; he might get one later. His mother was having old Mrs. Simpson over for afternoon tea. Perhaps he could sneak out then. He started writing again:

'That old injun medicine-man dunn cussed us pretty bad, Miss Mary. Gett'n the dead to rise, an' all.'

'Sure did, Sheriff. Cemetery must be 'bout empty by now, with all them dead folks walking the street.'

'Yeah, guess so. Help me drag this pew 'cross the door, then check on Father Gonzales. They bit him up someth'n terrible.'

Billy raised his head looking blindly at the window. Should he bring a Deputy Sheriff into the story, all the best westerns did? No, he wanted it to be bad! Gee, this was harder than he thought.

'Billy, lunch in half an hour,' his mother called. 'Don't you go anywhere!'

'OK, mum.'

He tasted plastic again and sighing, applied the pen to the paper.

Thursday morning was wet and dark. A chill wind blew early leaves across the slick playground and gusted under the classroom door. Brother Michael sat on his stool near the whiteboard wearing a black jumper over the obligatory white shirt. He cocked his head and regarded Billy without speaking, tapping his palm with a marker pen held in thin fingers. Like a magpie sizing up a worm, Billy thought trying to avoid the teacher's gaze.

He found his desk and threw himself onto the seat. Had all the compositions been marked? His heart sank as he noticed a pile of ill-matched pages on the teacher's desk, some with little squares of yellow paper along the edges. Would they be first? Billy suspected the old priest liked to be unpredictable. Perhaps it gave him a feeling of control.

Without preamble, Brother Michael stood and surveyed the class. Silence fell like a shroud. Billy wriggled uncomfortably as the first composition was chosen and the judgment began. *Not long now*, he thought.

The first few efforts were unremarkable in Billy's opinion. One was terrible; a girl sat sniffling. Sean was told to see Brother Michael after school; he looked unhappy.

'Terrance Ryan, stop gazing about and come and get your composition. And next time write it yourself!' said Brother Michael.

The morning stretched. Billy squirmed in his seat.

Lenny O'Brien threw a paper plane when heads were turned. It lay near the door fluttering occasionally in the draught.

Sally O'Connor got an **A** for a story about her sister's third birthday party that made Billy almost gag.

His heart sank; was his next?

'Sean Flynn, what are you trying to do? I can read yours this time. I gave you a **D**, for legibility.' The teacher smiled at his wit, his mouth a crooked slit below narrowed eyes.

There was still time then. Maybe another **C** would be fine.

111

'Now class, pay attention, I want to read you something,' said Brother Michael, his face a mask of authority.

Something wrong, he had never actually read anything before, was that good or bad? Billy's heart thumped as a composition was selected from the pile.

Brother Michael read:

Mary shrieked in terror as the doors of the church bulged inwards.

The sheriff fired uselessly as the stack of pews was swept aside and the dead entered. At first a few, then they crowded in the aisle and faced the three figures at the Alter. Father Gonzales gasped a prayer and held up his crucifix but it was brushed aside by a putrid hand.

Through the open doors Mary saw ragged forms shuffling towards them across the moonlit plaza as a low moaning sound rose from a hundred dead throats.

Suddenly there was a clap of thunder and a new sound. Indian drums beat a distant tattoo. In a flare of light a figure appeared: a creature of leather and feathers crouched in the dust, a staff in one hand and gourd rattle in the other. The undead stopped frozen as the old Indian stood. His painted face below a crown of buffalo horns swept back and forth as he stamped the earth and shook the rattle.

As Mary watched in dreadful fascination, he pointed his staff at the church and the tassel of eagle feathers at its tip fluttered as he began a slow circle, all the while shaking the gourd and chanting to that heathen beat.

As he turned, the goolish army collapsed into dust, each in its turn, as though pierced by a deadly ray. Another flash and silence returned to the village. When Mary next looked the plaza was empty.

Brother Michael put down the page. 'That's how it's done; and by the way Billy Galloway, you spell ghoul, "g-h-o-u-l," he added with a smile.

Billy knew he'd lost.

Coffee Casanova

'**G'day**, a cappuccino, please ... and your phone number.' He smiled his most winning smile, 'I'm Andy.'

'And I'm busy,' Karen brushed aside an errant red hair from her oval face and reached for a paper cup as she fixed him with blue eyes below a furrowed brow.

'Have here or take away?'

'Take away! There's a good show at the Cremorne Orpheum,' he said, his voice rising.

Andy was arrogant and vain, but believed these flaws balanced his dark good looks, bright disposition and wit. He was almost universally well liked.

'$3.50, please.'

'Heh, come on, it's a French film I'm sure you'd like it, it's full of romantic female stuff.'

He handed her a $5 note.

Karen worked with Shirley in their coffee-and-cake stall squeezed between two bank buildings on lower George Street. *Café Belle* drew lunchtime crowds who happily queued past the unused table on the footpath to place their coffee orders between the cake displays. Shirley was known for her skill as a barista; Karen played her part by shining her sunny personality and auburn-framed smile into the street on the gloomiest of days.

The machine hissed and gurgled as a jug of milk was frothed. Karen marked a plastic cap and handed it to Shirley at the machine. Shirley met her eyes and laughed.

'$1.50, thank you,' said Karen.

Andy felt their hands brush as she handed him the change.

'Next please!' she said, looking over his shoulder.

Shirley clipped the plastic cap onto his cup and placed it on the glass case.

Where had he gone wrong?

He turned from the counter warming his hands on the cup and raised it for a quick sip. Then he noticed the scribbled note in blue ink, "Cap. 0057 334 902."

Andy smiled in happy satisfaction.

David and the Man

Light came; a door slammed in the street below; no school today. David stirred in his warm nest; the day was beginning. More sounds rose from the street, the low rumble of many wheels on concrete. Resisting the morning chill, he stood on his bed and pushed aside the curtains. The sound made the tinny scrape of thin curtain rings on metal. Dawn, low and bright, lit the rooftops and chimneys in a vivid glow, cutting around the angular shapes to leave sharp dew-soaked shadows on the slate.

David's fingers fumbled hastily with shorts and shirt, leaving the occasional button for future adjustment. No thought was required or expected. The day was calling and David obeyed. No shoes, no coat. His feet made soft padding sounds, skin on polished floorboards, as he left his room. No sound came from the kitchen yet. More awake now, he stepped to the front door. He was careful to turn the knob slowly, but the soft scrape of metal on metal sounded loud in the hallway. He held the knob against turning, quietly pulled the door shut, and turned to face the stairs. He'd escaped. He hurried on. How could he be stopped by a call he could not hear?

Flying now, he leaped from step to step: two, three at a time. How fast could he go down to the street?

Suddenly he checked his downward plunge, gripping the wooden handrail in confusion. Even with a strong grasp, he almost tripped on the large battered bicycle spread on the stairs below. *This is something new. Mr. Williams never leaves his bike there; it's always in the foyer, under the stairs.*

He continued downward, stepping carefully through the bicycle frame and around the canted handlebars until he reached the bottom step.

The foyer seemed empty, yet the door was partly open and early light spread across the red tiles, lighting the stairs and the dark timber banister. His nose wriggled - a puzzling but familiar smell - as he peered into the gloomy space where the bicycle was usually kept.

At first, his mind would not register what he saw, then it clicked into understanding: a large pile of cardboard and papers. Familiar enough, but why? The smell was stronger. Then the pile moved, a slithering, heaving motion that spread its edges further.

David jumped back in alarm! *A rat? A snake?* He knew about rats; he'd seen a dead one in the street once. He didn't know much about snakes though. *Could they jump?*

A man's head appeared: long hair, grey, pasty, unshaven. Pale bloodshot eyes regarded him silently for an instant, then blinked.

'Hello, who are you?' said the man.

Silence.

'Do you live here?'

'My name's David, I live in number six with my mother. I came down to get the bread,' the words gushing out like a blocked hose suddenly released. 'Who are you? What are you doing here? Mr. Williams' bike should be here.'

117

He realised now the smell was coming from the man.

'Have you got anything to drink?'

'No,' said David, his thirst aroused. 'I have to go now. *Gặp lại sau nhé,*' he said, turning away.

The man stiffened, 'What did you say?'

'I said *Gặp lại sau nhé.* It's Vietnamese. It means ...'

'It means "See you later",' interrupted the man.

'Yes, how did you know?' said David.

'Where did you learn that?' asked the man softly, ignoring the question.

'Mr. Phuong at the bread shop taught me. He's from Vietnam,' said David, getting a little worried, though rather intrigued. *Was it a rude thing to say?*

A second passed. The front door slammed as someone else left the building. They didn't bother looking under the stairs.

'When Mr. Phuong gives you the bread, tell him *Chào ông,* can you remember that?'

'Of course,' said David indignantly, repeating the phrase flawlessly. 'Have you been in Vietnam?'

'Yes, a long time ago.'

'Can you speak Vietnamese?'

'I could do many things once,' said the man, pausing; 'now I can't do anything. Off you go. Don't keep your mother waiting.'

David backed out the door, watching the man curiously as he turned and ran quickly down the street.

There was much to tell his friend, Mr. Phuong, this morning.

The day was still young when David reached the shop. It was just as well. There was nobody around as David burst in and gushed out his story. At one point, Mr. Phuong had to stop him to suggest he try breathing before he continued. 'He said to say, *Chào ông*' to you,' said David finally. 'What does it mean?'

'Oh, it just means 'hello,'" said Mr. Phuong, and then he was silent, looking into the distance like David's mother did when she was remembering his father.

'Do you know him?' asked David.

'I knew many men from Australia. It was a long time ago. We were all very young.'

Finally he said softly and seriously, 'David, here is your mother's bread. And here is something for your friend under the stairs.' He gathered up a fresh loaf of bread and a can of soft drink and put it in a plastic bag. 'Please tell him *thank you* from me and my family,' he said.

David did not really understand.

He knew something serious had happened.

Adults were like that sometimes.

But he was already late, so he simply fare-welled Mr. Phuong and ran out the door. He wanted to deliver the package and tell him what Mr. Phuong had said, but when he looked under the stairs, the man had gone.

Murder in Progress

'**Come** in,' the voice was male, sharp and impatient.

Imran pushed the heavy door and entered. The room was large and dim. A stranger could've been unsettled by its size, but Imran had been here before. He grasped his briefcase in both hands, gathered his courage and headed for the desk at the other end.

'Ah, it's you. Sit down, Imran. We need to talk,' the speaker was a large man with a florid oval face. He remained seated and waved Imran to the only seat available before glancing back to the file on his desk. Imran sank into the seat's plush comfort and observed again how he could barely see over the expansive desktop. A deliberate attempt at intimidation! *How juvenile.*

'God, Imran. What are you doing? This latest of yours: *A Dark and Deadly Secret?* It's rubbish, Imran. Really, right from the beginning! Couldn't you have found a more clichéd title?' he smirked and didn't wait for a reply. 'And the plot: unbelievable! Even with the wildest imagination who would believe an author could hate his publisher so much he'd murder him in such a calculated way, and get away with it? Ridiculous! Where's the hook, the climax, the denouement, the crisis and redemption or something. Nothing.'

Imran tried to get a word in, 'Well it was only a first draft, Mr. Ransom. An outline really ...'

'And then there are the characters.' Ransom fixed him with a direct stare. 'There are only two, but you still couldn't get it right. The publisher: a puffed up, overweight, caricature of a publishing tycoon, perpetually ranting. Who could believe such an unrealistic character?'

Imran did not reply, concluding the question was merely rhetorical.

'And the author, the protagonist; who were you thinking of? James Bond? Six feet, dark, debonair; speaks five languages and a champion bridge player.' He fixed Imran with another stare.

Imran leant forward raising himself over the desktop.

'Well, my mother ...' he started, yet Ransom was not listening.

'And finally, the murder: lethal skin contact with a handshake? Good heavens, Imran. That sort of stuff went out with the cold war. It's so much '60s.'

'But there are such poisons,' protested Imran. 'Take the antidote; shake hands; victim dies in a few weeks. Couldn't be easier! Untraceable. The Russians ...'

'*Never mind* the Russians, Imran! This is the end. You haven't written a publishable story in months. We can't carry you forever. I just called you in out of courtesy, to let you know the directors have agreed. We cannot publish your stories any longer. I hope you understand.'

He paused for the first time and looked Imran in the eye.

'I'm sorry you feel this way, Mr. Ransom. I tried to explain on the phone. I'm just going through a dry spell, it happens to all writers. I'm sure you know. Change a few words and I could be famous in a few months, people will clamour for my stories. I'm sure the directors will be delighted.'

'Delighted … delighted! How can you know that? Do you actually have some dark secret magic? Something you haven't been telling me, Imran? No, the directors agree, you're a useless no-talent. A one-book wonder. No, Imran. I'm sorry… '

Imran, heaved himself forward. It took two tries to get out of the chair, but finally he rose to his full height.

Ransom waited for his parting words.

'Implausible characters, eh. You fat fool.' Ransom's jaw dropped in surprise. 'You can't even recognise yourself when it's pushed in your face. Implausible plot, eh? You'll change your mind in a few weeks. You're right on one score; there was no denouement in the story, no final drawing together of all the threads. I wasn't sure about how to finish it, but I have that now. I just need to write it up.'

He stretched across the desk and thrust his hand at the publisher. Ransom took it again in a desultory reflex motion, a puzzled look on his face.

Imran turned towards the door. Silence followed him across the carpet. He put his hand on the knob and turned, smiling. 'Yes, *A Dark and Deadly Secret*, it is quite a cliché. Perhaps you'd prefer the alternative title I have: Dead Man Walking.

'Good bye Mr. Ransom

Death Warmed Up

'Not much to tell really, I put the key in the lock, and pushed open the door. I felt like a burglar in someone else's house. The air was warm, a little hot actually. There was a philodendron in the hallway and I knew there must be other plants, so I headed for the back to find a watering can. That's when I saw the body. All that blood; with blood all over his head like in some cheap detective story! I could see he was dead so I called 000, and waited for your lot to turn up. Is this the detail you want? I'm sorry; I'm just a bit shocked, officer. Who could've done this?'

'It's Detective, actually, Mr. White; Detective Carol, but don't worry about that.'

He seemed too young to be a detective yet wore a dark suit and black shoes with rounded toes, so I should've known.

'How did you come to be here in the first place?' he continued. And so it went for most of the morning.

What a shit time of my life that was! I'd lost everything by being stupid, and now all I had was cold dinners and Classic movies. On that particular day, I arrived home from the office about 6.30. It was Monday. I remember thinking it was three weeks to my next birthday. I'd only moved into my new house the day before. Something small because I didn't have much left after the divorce. Trying to convince myself this was what I wanted, I'd just settled down with the latest *Modern Movie* magazine and a glass of *Yarra Valley red* as a chill August wind howled around the eaves.

When the phone rang, I was not pleased.

'Hello, this is Bob Willis, Mr. White. We haven't met. I'm your next-door neighbour, at № 26.'

'Oh, hello," I said, mentally urging him to get on with it.

'Err, yes, I wondered whether I could ask you to do a small favour for me? I'm going on a trip tomorrow, haven't travelled for years though I'm a bit freer now. There's nobody else in the house … . I just wondered if you would mind watering my indoor plants and emptying my mailbox while I'm away?' his voice rising in a question. 'I'm sorry I'm not very organised and I don't know who else to ask. It'll only be a couple of weeks.'

I let his confession stand while I considered for a moment. Perhaps it would help me to establish myself in the area. God knows, I had few friends left.

Do the neighbourly thing. Be the good neighbour.

He sounded about my age; maybe we could have a glass of red together when he got back. I must admit I'd felt a bit isolated since I split with Sonya … .

'Yeah, OK. I'll need a key. Where are you going on your trip?'

'That's wonderful, thanks very much. I'll put a key in your letterbox tonight. If you could go in tomorrow when you come home, that would be good; and then about one week later. I'm going north to escape the winter, somewhere in Queensland. I'd better go now though; I have a lot of packing to do. I'm afraid I left it too late. Thanks very much again,' and he hung up.

I put the phone down and settled back with my glass of red. *A bit abrupt*, I thought, *but some people are like that; I'd keep an open mind until I meet him in a couple of weeks.*

Later, Lance Burgess came around and we put a DVD in the player. It was "The Third Man," I think. Lance is a good friend and didn't ask any questions, just sat and watched the movie with me. Soon I'd pushed Bob Willis and his plants to the back of my mind.

In the morning, I remembered my promise, then realised I'd be going directly from my office to a screening of The 39 Steps at the Orpheum and would not be able to water Willis's plants as arranged. That's when I decided to do the job before I went to work … and so found myself in my neighbour's kitchen with Detective "round-toes" Carol, shaking like a leaf and trying not to chuck on the lino

'Was it a burglary; a home invasion; something gone wrong, Const … Detective Carol?'

'What makes you say that?' he asked in a low voice as he leaned towards me, frowning.

'Well, I … I … just assumed … with the place in a mess like it is … all the drawers open … papers everywhere …'

'We're not jumping to conclusions, Mr. White. There are a few items to consider. For example: how did the killer get in? Who had a key? What other motives could there be?'

His blue eyes considered me as he paused, waiting for my reply. 'You don't think I killed him, surely? I told you I never met Willis. We only spoke on the phone. I don't know anything about him. Perhaps he knew the killer and let him in. There are many possibilities. And I certainly didn't have any reason to kill him.'

I realised I'd half risen to my feet.

Detective Carol replied in a soft voice, 'I believe you, Mr. White. The fact is we know you didn't do it. You have an alibi for the time of death. You were watching a DVD with a friend, I understand. From the condition of the body, we think he died around midnight on Monday. It's only preliminary, of course.'

It didn't take long for the guilt to set in. I couldn't get the image of the dead man out of my mind. He must've been killed while Lance and I were drinking our wine, lying there only metres away while I slept.

The scene kept repeating itself in my head.

I remembered pushing open the garden gate, and then pictured Bob Willis on a coach ride to Cooktown. A portly figure in jeans and white t-shirt. A Crocodile Dundee hat above a florid city face. The t-shirt has a stenciled road sign and the words "Beware of Crocs" emblazoned across his chest.

Having never met him, I could imagine anyone I liked.

Curious how trusting some people can be!

Perhaps he already knew about me through my books before he rang? Or thought he did. I should've asked more questions. I just thought I'd learn soon enough.

How wrong could I be?

I went to the house; I put my foot on the first sandstone step and fumbled for the brass key I'd found in my letterbox that morning. The veranda floorboards appeared original 1938 hardwood. Hard to replace.

I raised the key and inserted it in the lock …

The scene repeated like a film loop.

When would it stop!

But I wasn't finished with Detective Carol.

'Tell me more about the telephone call, Mr. White. You'd never spoken to Mr. Willis. How did you know who it was? Did the caller sound young or old? Was he nervous?

Did he say anything else you can remember? Did you take the call on your home phone, or mobile?'

'I've told you everything I can remember. Why wouldn't it be Bob Willis? He sounded about my age. He didn't sound at all nervous. Perhaps a little rushed, I assumed that was because he had to pack. The call was on my home phone, I don't give out my mobile number.'

'Why would Bob Willis have your phone number?'

'I don't know, he must've found out my name somehow then looked up the number. It didn't occur to me to ask at the time. The Real Estate Agent, Fred Lurks, is the only one who would've known.

'Who the hell was Bob Willis anyway? Why would anyone kill him?'

The detective's long face took on a more animated expression I couldn't at first interpret, before the corners of his mouth drooped in an ironic smile.

'You should leave the detective work to us, Mr. White; but you're right. Who is Bob Willis? Well, we know who he is not! He is not the dead man in the lounge.'

He lent back and observed me with something like amusement, while I listened slack-jawed.

'His name is Anvil Jarik. He is, or *was*, a drug dealer and petty thief. We'd like to know why he was in the house. Perhaps your neighbour can tell us, when we find him.'

Thinking back, I don't know why I didn't punch him. He'd kept me in the dark while he milked me for information; considering me a possible suspect. Of course, it made perfect sense.

I'd never met Willis and it was easy to assume it was his body. How long would it take Detective Carol to presume I could've made up the whole story!

Would he continue looking for Bob Willis?

I didn't have long to wait; he rang me in my office the next day.

'I thought you'd like to know, Queensland police have arrested Robert Willis. He tried the burglary line but finally confessed when presented with the evidence. It seems they were in the drug business. Willis handled the importing and bookkeeping and Jarik looked after the distribution. Willis covered his tracks with his Real Estate business, but after his wife and kids left him, he wanted out. Jarik wouldn't have it. They argued. Willis claims Jarik attacked him first, but Willis killed him with the vase. He tried to make us believe he left the house hours before. He rang you to set up his alibi. He might have got away with it too, if not for you.'

'Me? What did I do?'

'Well, we already had our suspicions; but you broke his alibi by going to the house too early. The warm air you noticed when you opened the door, you see; it should've been cool in the morning, not hot. He'd set the air conditioning temperature "high" and put it on a six hour timer. It's the body temperature; we calculated the time of death to be at least six hours later than it actually was. When I heard your story, I checked the air conditioning and his whole story fell apart. If you'd entered the house in the afternoon, it would have been cooler. You were meant to give him an alibi but you caught him out in the end. Thank you for helping us to catch a killer.'

I still felt guilty.

I had grudgingly offered to help someone but couldn't even get that right, so I simply said,

'No need to thank me, Detective, I was just being a good neighbour.'

The Seer

Arthur swirled his teacup again and watched the leaves settle. They formed interesting hieroglyphs and strange shapes against the white porcelain, but nothing he recognised. Nothing that could tell him what to do next. He sighed and put the cup down.

He wasn't in a good mood, he decided. His new accommodation was proving less than satisfactory and he hadn't slept well. The bathroom taps dripped and the noises from his neighbours' rooms not only disturbed his sleep, but also raised troubling questions about their activities.

He scratched his unshaven chin and finished his corn flakes. He had to concede some of the decisions he'd made recently were not good. It wasn't his fault he decided, it was just fate.

He sighed again.

All a young bloke needs is a few breaks, he said to himself with forced humour. Reduced to cornflakes and the local newspaper, *The Mosman Daily* would have to do until he set up a new delivery account for *The Herald*.

At least it's free, he thought.

He made himself another cup of tea and settled down to read. The first few pages were filled with unfamiliar local news and real estate he could not afford. He decided to look for a new dentist and flicked to page 57; and that's when he saw it.

It was in *Psychic Notices and Astrology*, just below *Adult Services:*

WHAT DOES YOUR FUTURE HOLD?
MADAM CHENG KNOWS.
FIND LOVE OR FORTUNE.
MR. BRUMBLE PLEASE CALL URGENTLY
ABOUT YOUR FUTURE
APPOINTMENTS ONLY

Arthur stopped reading and held his breath, astonished to see his name in print. What is this? A fortuneteller knows my name? Ah, of course, it must be someone else, another person. There are plenty of Brumbles in the phonebook. With a sigh of relief, he returned to his cup of tea and his search of "D for Dentist."

But it would not rest.

What if it is for me?

He knew it was impossible yet the thought wouldn't leave him. *What if this silly woman, Madam Cheng, really knows something; strange things are possible!*

He stood, pushing his chair back with a clatter, crossed the room, and jerked the phone from the kitchen bench top. He dialled the number, all thought of the new dentist now forgotten.

'Good morning, Madam Cheng's Rooms,' said a pleasant female voice of indeterminate age. 'How can I help you?'

Rooms! Rooms! What next!

'I'd like to speak to Madam Cheng, please,' he said without warmth.

'This is Madam Cheng, Mr. Brumble. Would you like to make an appointment?'

'I'd like to know about your ad in *The Mosman Daily*. Am I the person you're looking for?' said Arthur tersely;

How could she know my name?

'I'm sorry Mr. Brumble,' sounded the even reply. 'I don't do readings over the telephone. I do have a vacancy tomorrow though, if you would like to come and see me?'

'Surely,' he said, anger rising, 'you can just tell me whether I'm the person you're looking for, and save us both a lot of time?'

'The future is not something to be taken lightly, Mr. Brumble. Fate has allowed me a small glimpse through the curtain of time. If you are interested in your future, you really should come and see me.'

He considered this briefly; poppycock of course, but what harm would it do to find out more. He could tell a scam a mile away and he could certainly smell one here. 'What will it cost?' he asked.

'What would you pay to know your future, Mr. Brumble?' she replied. 'I have a unique gift, but I offer it to the world at a very reasonable price. My usual fee is $50 a session.' She stopped, 'but yours is a special case,' she continued before he could say anything. 'I sense you are unsure. This is what I'll do. If you're not impressed by what I tell you, there will be no charge.'

Arthur considered.

He was still suspicious, though what harm could it do?

At worst, he would waste his time. At best, who knows? 'Oh, all right. When can I see you?'

'Tomorrow morning at 10.15, if that's convenient.'

She gave him the address.

'All right, 10.15 tomorrow; and I hope you have some answers, goodbye!'

'Goodbye, Mr Brumble. See you tomorrow,' she added brightly.

The next day was overcast and dreary when Arthur caught the bus to Chatswood.

He was beginning to hate this damned woman.

She knew things about him and claimed to know his future. How was that possible?

He must see her and put this matter to rest.

Madam Cheng's "rooms" were in an old-style brick office building near the town centre. He walked to the door and the light of the street fell away as he entered and took the creaking lift to the third floor. A sign directed him to the left and he searched impatiently along the gloomy corridor. Finally, gold letters on a pearl glass panel proclaimed the number and the words, "Madam Cheng".

He pushed open the door and a bell sounded somewhere in another room. The small waiting room was empty. He waited for a few seconds and was about to seat himself on a heavily-brocaded settee when an inner office door opened abruptly and a small slim middle-aged Asian woman appeared.

The preconceived ideas Arthur had about Madam Cheng abruptly fell apart. This was no thin-faced gypsy woman with headscarf and crystal ball. Madam Cheng was conservatively dressed in a black business suit of stylish cut; her straight black hair wound into a bun at the back of her head.

She wore little or no makeup and a pair of glasses hung on a cord around her neck, *more like an accountant.*

Arthur had been expecting more.

She offered her hand. 'I'm Audrey Cheng,' she said pleasantly with no hint of an accent.

'Arthur Brumble,' he mumbled reluctantly.

She did not release his hand immediately. Holding it with both of hers she looked over his shoulder into the distance. Arthur found this very disconcerting, but before he could react, she released him and broke the awkward silence. 'Please come into my office Mr. Brumble. You and I have quite a lot to talk about.'

Arthur's disquiet mounted.

He had no alternative, but to follow her.

Madam Chengs' office was not large. The only furniture he could see were several ornately-decorated screens, a small leather-topped table and two strange-looking wooden chairs with arms and legs carved into grotesque depictions of dragons and fish. Thick crimson curtains trimmed the windows.

'Please sit down Mr. Brumble,' indicating one of the chairs and seating herself in the other.

Arthur decided he needed to take control of the situation. 'What do you think you know about my future?' he demanded as he sat down.

She did not respond to the implied scepticism.

'Oh, first things first, Mr. Brumble", she smiled.

She sat upright, her hands folded in her lap. 'Time begins with the present. I know you are Arthur Brumble, and you live in Crows Nest,' she stated in a friendly but definite manner.

'Yes, yes, I told you that on the phone,' he interrupted.

'But you didn't tell me you'd previously lived in Lane Cove, are recently divorced and that you missed out on a promotion at work, did you?' She replied calmly.

He jerked backwards in his chair, his jaw dropped open in amazement, and his eyes widened.

'Yes, how did ...?

'I've been given many powers, Mr. Brumble; your life is not a mystery to me. Would you like to hear more?' she smiled.

Arthur's heart pumped, he gripped the arms of the chair, his eyebrows arched. *She does know*! Now he would finally find what life really owed him.

'Yes, of course,' he said earnestly, 'what … what can you tell me?'

'I know several months ago you made a decision that will have a big impact on your future.' She spoke softly, putting her hands on the desk, cupping them together.

Arthur lent forward expectantly.

She could only be talking about his shares!

There will be a takeover or something and he will make a huge windfall profit!

That must be it!

'Last year you had $10,000 worth of oral reconstruction work done, but you moved away without paying your dentist.'

She slipped a small envelope across the desk to him. 'That dentist was Geoffrey Lee, my nephew. You need to pay his bill immediately, Mr. Brumble,' she said.

A long period of silence followed.

Arthur saw his visions of wealth collapsed about him.

'Otherwise your future is very clear indeed, Mr. Brumble. Would you like another appointment?'

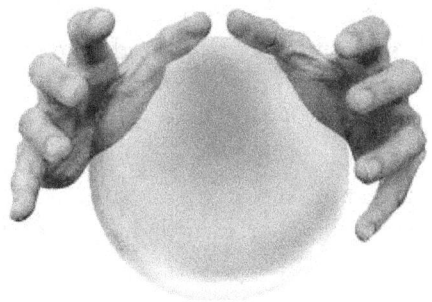

A Gift Returned

'So, Dalon, what is your decision?'

'My decision stands, Lord Saran. I will not support you. The Earth Bender's Council is too important to have a self-serving egotist as President. You would be a disaster.'

Saran drew his black cloak closer about his thin frame. Dalon marveled again how much like an underfed raven he looked, even his long black hair falling in one swoop to his collar, supported the appearance.

'You were never one to mince your words, Dalon. You are also an arrogant young fool. The Council will meet in this very room in two days. It is divided; your vote would decide the matter. On the other hand, if you are not present, others might see reason and turn to my side. That old fool, Alendarl will soon be gone, and you with him.'

The younger man faced him calmly. The simplicity of his blue jerkin and white kilt would've revealed him as a scribe of lower rank, were it not for the richness of the fabric. His hair was gathered into an auburn topknot, in the manner of the outer lands.

"Is that a threat, Lord Saran?"

'How perceptive of you, Dalon.' He smiled briefly then pursed his lips, a low whistle arose, seeming to fill the Chamber. As he whistled he held up his hand and a white cloud appeared to coalesce and grow at his fingertips. The nebulus ball of opal white continued to expand as he cast it at Dalon's chest. The gasp that arose from Dalon's throat was absorbed in the swirling fog.

He was lost, blinded in a white universe.

He turned to run, just as the swirling whiteness began to clear as quickly as it had appeared.

He could see his knees again. The thinning cloud became a mist through which he could make out dark shapes. Objects appeared dimly, trees, rocks, now he could see pale ground beneath his feet.

The solid parquetry of the Council Chamber floor had gone replaced by the soft sound of a calm tide as he stood on white sand and shell grit. He stumbled to the nearest rock, his legs trembling. Saran had revealed himself and used his gift to send Dalon into exile.

But to where?

'Lord Saran, I must protest. This haste is not appropriate for such an important occasion.' The speaker ran his thin fingers through his white beard and lent heavily on a thick wooden staff taller than himself.

'Alendarl, do not concern yourself with speed. I expect at your age most things appear hasty and ill-considered, but our council needs able guidance. Some of our *sensitives* have seen bad omens. Dangerous times may be upon us. We need to prepare with strong leadership.'

'Omens? What rubbish is this, Saran? Need I remind you we each have a gift? A power we don't understand. Twelve centuries ago, none had what we have. Then our new kind began to appear, few and rare. We are gifted with strange abilities. Omens and superstitious signs play no part: we can or we cannot; we know or we know not.'

The effort seemed to drain the old man and he slumped in his chair.

'Pah! Enough talk, Alendarl. The Council has decided, tomorrow at noon we vote for a new President.'

The unnatural fog had completely lifted. The sky above was grey and sunless. Dalon sat on a rocky outcrop above a narrow beach. At the edge of the sand sharp rocks poked through and the land rose steeply, covered in stunted wind-sculptured trees. On his left and right, the rugged coast disappeared from sight. He rose and followed the light breeze regardless of its direction.

The day grew warmer as he walked. Each view of the sand, rocks and trees seemed identical to the next. No sign of human presence marked the scene. He was tired and wracked with thirst.

He was preparing to leave the beach and seek the shelter of the trees when a shape in the sand drew his attention. He recognised the footprints he'd made several hours before. He'd come full circle.

He slumped again onto the same rock he had sat on before, and viewed the beach and grey sea before him.

A movement between water and rock broke his reverie. A silent puff of cloud appeared and grew swiftly into a ball of swirling milkiness that flowed over the sand to his feet and towered above him, then, almost as quickly as it grew, it began to retreat. The turbulent opal ball held its shape but at its centre appeared something solid. Its vague outline became a figure, a man, no, a slim youth.. or, he gasped in astonishment as a girl in a green tunic stepped from the remaining tatters of cloud. She wore purple tights and a wide belt and her long hair was the colour of the sun. She looked in his direction with wide eyes and screamed.

'Why has Saran called this meeting, Lord Alendarl? Are we to be summonsed like lowly norms, when he finds it convenient?' The little man spat the words with derision.

'I would lower your voice if I were you, Nandar. Lord Saran would not appreciate your anger,' replied Alendarl.

'And what is that to me, Alendarl. Why do you fear him? Surely, all here are to be trusted. We govern for the good of all in Kandari.'

'Yes, and I fear Saran would govern us, "for the good." Do not be deceived, Nandar, he is a dangerous man. Strange things have been happening lately. Already several council members have disappeared; including my nephew, Dalon, who's spoken against Saran often in the past. Be cautious.'

Dalon regarded the girl with unguarded suspicion. 'Who are you; and why did Saran send you here?' he asked.

'I am Mata, daughter of Tenerik, Master of Wohndor. Our lands lie within Lord Saran's realm and he would add our estate to his title. He tried to take me as his third wife, but I refused. He was very angry and used his gift to send me here.'

'You are high-born then, Mata. Do you also have a gift?'

'Since very young, I am one with the beasts of the earth and creatures of sky and sea. They listen to my will and obey me.' Dalon smiled for the first time and took her hand in his.

'Then Mata, daughter of Tenerik, prepare yourself; we will leave here soon and Lord Saran will regret his arrogance. But first, we need to know where we are. Can you find a winged friend to locate our island prison from above?'

'That, and more, friend Dalon! Wait for me here.' She stood and walked to the water's edge. The gulls on the sand suddenly rose as one, squawking in confusion, circling above her, forming a flock that rose in ever widening circles into the sky.

<hr/>

'Bailiff, shut the doors. The Council of Earth Bender's of Kandari is now in session. You all have a copy of our agenda ...'

'Mr. President!'

'Lord Saran, you have something to say?'

'My Lord and Honourable Councillors, may I suggest a suspension of the normal order of business so we may conduct the election? This is surely the most important matter of the day.'

'Well, I ...'

A murmur of assent rose from the chamber.

Saran has prepared them well, thought Alendarl.

He spoke in a loud clear voice that reached to the highest ranks of the chamber without apparent effort. 'Councillors, I have led this Council for the last five years. In that time we have made many changes for the benefit of Kandari. Many of you think me weak and slow and perhaps it is time for a new leader. However, we have missing members from this chamber; fine lords who've not been seen in recent weeks, those who cannot be contacted. Should we not delay until they return?'

'Lord Alendarl,' spoke Saran, and the chamber grew silent. 'No one can say when these Councillors will return. We need to be decisive. We need to get on with the business of governing Kandari. Delaying such matters will only make things worse. I say we proceed directly to the vote.'

He paused, about to continue, when his presentation was interrupted by a loud knocking at the tall wooden doors. A puzzled silence fell, and all eyes turned in concern towards the entrance to the chamber. Before anyone could react, one of the doors burst inward, torn from its hinges by some tremendous force. It fell forward and the draught from its toppling blew papers from a dozen benches in the tiered ranks.

Into a shocked circle of Councillors and officials stepped Dalon, his long hair flying, his red face smeared with sweat and dust.

'*Stop!* Lord President, I interrupt proceedings to prevent a huge injustice. I accuse a man - a Lord no less - of heinous crimes. Kidnapping and attempted murder. That man stands among you, as Lord Saran. Saran, the Duplicitous: who used his gift, to kidnap - and murder - in an attempt to control this Council. A man ...'

"Must I stand and be accused by this boy of foul crimes without a chance to defend myself? What proof of these crimes do you have Dalon? Who have I murdered, who have I kidnapped?"

Dalon lifted his eyes to the assembly, each member leaning forward to be part of the action below.

My Lords, Lord Saran used his gift to transport me to an island of exile and starvation. He has deceived us all. He spreads a cloak of righteous concern over a murderous heart. But you need not believe me alone. I introduce my rescuer, the Lady Mata, daughter of Tenerik, Master of Wohndor, who also has been foully used by Lord Saran.'

Dalon's words, delivered with sharp skill and irony, appeared to pierce Saran like a blade. His face paled as though drained of blood as his black cloak fluttered in the draught from the shattered door.

As Mata strode across the broad chamber floor, Saran stumbled forward a few paces his mouth agape. As the assembly watched in stunned silence, he stopped and straightened, his face a mask of malice. Swinging about he caught Dalon's eye and raised his hand. A low whistle escaped his lips as a small cloud began to grow at his fingertips. Dalon was prepared. Holding up both palms towards the fallen lord, his lips moved in silent incantation.

Saran froze, his body no longer his servant.

He watched in mute terror as his white cloud grew larger, obscuring him from view as the crowded assembly struggled to see him through the opal ball.

Dalon held his deadly pose as the swirling mist began to disipate.

Saran was nowhere to be seen.

Bob the Barber.

The barbershop was two chairs and a cash register squeezed between "Shoe Repairs" and a graffitied door. Light spilt into the gloomy arcade with garish intent, no need for a sign. A man covered by a blue cape occupied one chair. Behind him crouched the barber with long scissors.

I pushed at the door; it squealed in protest and allowed me into a thick atmosphere of hot air and cologne. The barber ignored me while the man in the chair followed my movements in the mirror lining one wall. Dolly Parton sang a wistful melody from somewhere.

The barber was short and thin, his grey hair cropped short. His white jacket flopped open to reveal a chequered shirt. I picked up a magazine and turned it to admire the centrefold. Before I could begin, the barber straightened.

'How does that look?' he said handing the man a small mirror. The man examined himself for a long moment seeing something invisible to others.

'Yeah, that's good,' he said, lying or deluded.

The cape disappeared with a flourish and the customer stood, reaching for his wallet as the barber produced a small brush and applied it with small unctuous strokes.

I moved uninvited to the still warm seat and waited. Payment completed the barber turned to me.

'G'day, how's your day been?' I felt his breath as his twin moved his lips in the mirror.

'Yeah ... not bad so far,'

'How would you like it?'

'Oh, a number two all over,' I said, 'part it on the right,' adding wit at the last-minute. The arcane society of the barbershop seemed to demand humour and bright repartee. But he ignored it, flapping the blue cape a couple of times and spreading it over me.

I felt like a Christmas turkey as he secured it at my neck.

'What have you been up to?' he said as though to an old friend.

'Oh, I managed to scribble a few pages this morning.'

'Yer not one of those writer blokes, are you?' he said picking up clippers.

'Well, as a matter of ...'

Buzz, buzz!

A month's grey growth lay on the floor.

'All pooftas, the lot of them. They should be shot and worse! What did you write, a letter or something?'

He ducked and looked at my stubble from several angles.

'Er, no I write, ah ... . What don't you like about writers?'

He was using scissors now.

Long, sharp and close to my skull.

Snip, snip! 'Bloody trouble makers. Look what they wrote about the All Blacks.'

'Oh, you read the paper then?'

144

'What! No way; heard it on the radio. Alan Jones was talking about it.'

Snip, snip!

He put down the scissors and admired his handiwork.

'What did you say you were writing?' he asked, as he unfolded a pearl handled razor and stared at me in the mirror his eyes narrowed.

'Oh, er, taxation department ...,' I lied, 'you know, business stuff.'

Slap, slap!

He let the razor strop fall raising the gleaming blade. Subtle pressure from his fingers and I tilted my head exposing my side-lever - and my throat - to his blade.

'You don't read books then?' I said, trying to divert him from my disquiet.

'No way!' he said, jerking his head up and looking at me with a frown.

I tried to wriggle my right ear. I felt nothing.

'What about the Bible? I said, regretting it immediately.

Dolly's tune seemed a little off key. The razor scraped the nape of my neck as I put my chin to my chest. I looked for my ear among the scraps of hair and soiled tissues on the floor.

'Typical,' he said at last, 'just what I mean. A bunch of writers steal someone's ideas and write a book, years later, and people call them saints and give them all the credit!'

'Is there anything you like about writers?' I asked, in desperation.

'No, they're a shiftless, smelly, unkempt lot,' be said, 'and that's just the blokes - and they don't like hair cuts, either!', he said, reinforcing the point.

He undid the cape at my neck and swept it from me. I stood as he picked up a brush and brandished it at my chest.

'How is it you know so much about writers?' I asked. Afraid for a moment that he might see the irony in my question.

He paused in his brushing and looked at me in the mirror.

'Oh, when you marry one you learn real quick.' He said with a bitter laugh.

Seeing my expression, he continued. 'Yeah, my first wife, damm her. Some idiots reckon she was good at it too, but it was all a lot of rubbish.'

I realised a thought had been kindled; now it burst into flame.

'You're not 'Bob the Barber', are you?' I exclaimed in surprise.

'Yeah, she always denied it, but everybody knew.' I handed him a $20 note.

Ting! It disappeared into the cash register.

'But you're not a sex mad, cheating, drunk,' I said, feigning surprise.

'Not like she made out.' He said, lips narrowing with indignation as he handed me the change.

Lacking words, I mumbled a reply and turned to go.

9 to 5 stopped mid-beat for the first race at Flemington as I pushed at the door and stepped into the arcade. *Oh, how mighty is the pen,* I thought, *and how sweet its revenge.*

146

Who Am I?

**Ti-san** ran with the long tireless stride of a hunter. The quarry was long out of his sight but he would cross the ridge and meet the panicked herd as they followed the valley floor. He knew the wounded beasts would tire quickly and other predators would not respect his prior claim.

The ground turned from grass tussocks to scattered bushes and outcrops of stone. In places he was forced to leap from rock to rock as he scrambled up the slope. A stone rolled under his foot and he grunted as he almost lost his balance, running, slower now as he neared the top of the ridge. On the thinly wooded crest, he paused and looked for any sign of the herd. There it was; a faint smudge of brown dust where the river began to spread across the valley!

They were slower than he expected. He would meet them where the river turned again. He set off, more slowly now, down the other side.

At the bottom of the slope he crouched in the shade of a low Jamada bush and waited. The wide plain spread before him. If his calculations were correct, the wounded beasts would be ready to fall by the time they reached the crook of the river.

He was concentrating on the plain where the hills began to rise again, when the air not far in front of him began to move. A patch of vision as big as his hut began to shiver. The familiar grass tussocks and bushes began to blur as though he was looking at them through the rising heat from a campfire. He blinked in confusion and quickly glanced away. The plain and river stayed as solid as ever but the strange patch steadied and slowly began to coalesce, still shimmering, into a transparent solid shape.

He rose to his feet but it did not occur to him to try to escape.

The vehicle when it appeared had the appearance of irregular blocks of stone, white in colour, sharp and straight. It floated from the ground at the height of his knees. The air below it still shimmered in an unnatural way.

He could now see that it was about half an arrows flight from him. He reached behind and unslung his bow and quiver.

A voice spoke softly, 'Don't be afraid Tyson. This is Ali Williams. If you can understand me, we are here to pick you up. Just wait where you are.'

Now Ti-son was afraid.

The voice had spoken in his head. Was he possessed by a spirit? And how could it be that he could understand its words?

He looked around for the comforting presence of the others, but they were still following the herd far away. Wrapped in confusion he stood dumbly and waited.

Ti-San's heart was still racing when a loud click broke the silence and a figure stepped down from a hole in the vehicle. A woman. She was wearing a fine one-piece

148

garment, light blue in colour, that extended from her ankles to a high collar.

She strode towards him without hesitation.

How could he run from a woman? As she approached, he saw her lips move and heard her words. He started to listen. 'Yes,' she said. 'I ... talking ... out of it. ... remember me?' The sounds became clearer by the second.

'Who-are-you?' he said slowly in the language of his people.

'Dr. Alison Williams', the words sounded familiar but without meaning.

'Ali Williams', she repeated slowly, 'You know me. I'm ... your doctor. You've been very sick.'

'I am Ti-san. My father is ... is ... I can't remember.'

He shook his head in frustration.

'Don't *try*. Just *relax*.' She drew a small flask from her gown and held it towards him. 'It's OK. It's safe.' She took a short sip to demonstrate and offered it again.

'My father's name is ...', he said slowly.

Suddenly he was thirsty and reached for the flask. 'I can't remember ...'

'Listen to me carefully. You are not in danger. Your name is John Tyson. You are 32 years old. You are the son of Ron and Beryl Tyson. You were born in New Zealand and came here as a boy. You took an army scholarship at university and served four years before joining the security services. Your best friend's name was Barry Reynolds. Does any of this make sense to you?'

The liquid was bitter but refreshing. His head began to clear a little but he was still confused. He looked down at his hands and legs.

The person whose body he saw wore finely made leather shorts and woven grass sandals. The arms were lean and tattooed with strange designs. Large brown hands held a finely made reflex bow already strung and ready. As he watched, the bow fell to the ground, released by fingers that did not belong to him.

He stumbled and covered his face with his hands. 'I am ... John ... Ti-san. I... I. Where is my family?' He did not hear the reply as his vision faded and he passed into unconsciousness.

In a night full of dreams he smiled at his wife across a flickering fire. She was pregnant again and would soon deliver him a fine girl-child to make his family complete. Light spilled onto the wicker roof and walls. Across the hut, his oldest son, the quiet one, fumbled with the binding on a knife handle. His efforts were crude but Ti-san would show him how to do it tomorrow. The boy was growing fast.

Suddenly he frowned. A rustle behind him. He turned to the crude door in time to see it pushed open. A giant face appeared, a pale women's face with smiling painted lips. He turned to face her, and opened his eyes.

A room, pale, flat angular walls and ... roof. Strange light burst through bright holes above. He lay in soft comfort. A quiet humming like the sound of a distant shore surrounded him. He could not remember anything. He would wait and let his waking mind bring him into the world. He forced himself to extend his awareness, ... Yes, there were sounds outside but he could not make sense of them. Distant harsh mechanical sounds, then, a short snatch of human voice, the sudden muffled call of a large bird, disturbingly unrecognisable.

Yes, it was a room, but the light...? Ah, not holes in the roof but sources of brilliance called ... what?

Understanding was just beyond his reach.

He struggled, reviewing his surroundings for any clue.

His sleeping surface was raised from the floor.

Strange cords were fixed to his head.

His throat was dry and his chest ached. He felt hot and reached to throw off the covering. Another cord attached to his hand pierced the skin without pain. He plucked at the cords on his head and found they came away easily. He flung off the cover and struggled to step to the floor. Standing, he swayed on his feet as feeling grew in his legs.

Unfamiliar clothing clutched at him and his head spun. He steadied himself on a metal framework sending small phials and cups crashing to the floor.

A strident, pulsing alarm sounded and the door burst open.

A large young man in blue clothing entered hurriedly. Tyson looked at him in confusion, his mouth opened and he grasped for words. Finally, "What ... help ..." was all he could manage.

"You'll have to get back into bed, Mr. Tyson," the young man said evenly as he approached.

The figure by the bed stared at him in bewilderment. He understood the words but everything was wrong. Nausea rose in him and he leant forward to vomit, almost collapsing. Quickly the other man moved to steady him and seat him on the edge of the bed. A bowl was produced and Tyson vomited copiously.

He felt his mouth being wiped and shook himself free. 'Just lie back, Mr. Tyson and I'll make you more comfortable," he repeated.

Exhausted, Tyson did what he was told realising even as he did so, that he completely understood the strange man's words.

'My name is Charles, I'm your nurse.' He said as he poured a glass of water. 'I'm going to look after you until you leave here.' He held the glass and Tyson drank instinctively, greedily.

'How do you feel now?' Tyson's blue eyes followed him but he heard and understood with another part of his brain. A slight pause then, 'I'll ask the doctor whether we can remove that drip in your hand. It seems to be troubling you.'

Another pause.

'I understand that you have been on a very difficult job. Something to do with the brain or the mind. Wow, that must be scary! I'd rather be shot than have my brain tampered with. They told me to talk to you as much as possible. It's not hard for a bloke like me. Would you like some breakfast?'

Tyson did not reply but watched as Charles spoke quietly into a small box attached to his shirt. 'He's awake but very mixed up. Not saying anything yet. Send down some orange juice, porridge and eggs on toast. We'll see what he likes.'

The food arrived on a tray carried by a young women. Charles picked up something from the tray and showed him a small knife, fork and spoon in a transparent bag. Ripping open the bag he pulled out the spoon and put it in a bowl. 'The eggs are here. The cover's to keep them warm.' Charles explained. 'I'll leave you to it. Just call if you need me. Enjoy your breakfast.'

He left the room.

Hunger drove the confusion from his head as he surveyed the tray in front of him. The familiarity of the eating implements was reassuring. He lifted the spoon and prodded the surface of the first dish. It yielded and looked vaguely familiar but he put it aside and looked at the eggs. Here was something he recognised.

He attacked them ravenously.

He smelt the glass of white liquid. A duller sensation than he was familiar with but he was certain it was milk.

He drank it gratefully.

Dull thoughts swirled in his mind. Like two people in the same body. When he tried to speak the other tried also.

He could bring up two sets of memories, but which memories were his?

He tried to concentrate and review recent events. He'd been waiting for the herd of longan to appear when the vehicle arrived with the woman ... Ali Williams ... he knew her somehow. How was that possible? He would have to put any questions aside until he had more information.

He must observe and learn.

He looked around the room, at the cords and the strange flashing boxes. They now looked vaguely familiar. Not cords, wires and... tubes, yes, the one that had been in his arm, a tube. The other end still connected to a transparent bag.

He forced himself to stay in the present where dual memories did not exist. His eyes roamed the room consciously studying every item.

Strange knowledge came to him. Yes, that was a chair .... and that a window. It was getting faster now. Knowledge rushing in, curtains, doors, ... television. The last was now familiar, he realised, but he could not remember what its purpose.

He pushed back the covers more carefully this time and stepped from the bed again. He did not rush, forcing himself to stay calm and continue the mental survey of his surroundings.

He took an unsteady step from the bed and almost fell, stood and shuffled towards the furthest door where Charles and the girl had entered.

His hands had an unconscious familiarity with the mechanism but the door would not open. Moving to the second door, he found that it was a cupboard. His leather shorts, and sandals were neatly stored on shelves but his bow, quiver, and knife were nowhere to be seen.

The third door revealed a strange small room. He swayed for a moment as familiarity rushed into his mind. Toilet, shower, water, mirror.

The last revealed a long face with olive brown skin and blue eyes. The head was covered in short stubble and the chin was smooth. As he watched the face slipped into familiarity and became his own. He realised with surprise that they must have shaved him while he slept.

Fumbling he used the toilet.

Ali Williams was standing by his bed. 'Hi Tyson, I heard you were up. I need to talk to you.' Tyson listened dumbly. 'There is an emergency and we haven't time for the niceties. So we need to explain a few things to you now. Are you up to it?' He had no idea what she could be talking about, but he nodded.

'Our country, your country, is at war with an intractable enemy.' She continued. 'We've had a few setbacks and we suspected a spy. We decided to plant someone inside their security forces; someone who could find the name of our traitor.' She paused briefly, and then continued. 'That person was you.

'You were almost immediately captured. You weren't physically tortured - *they have more subtle mental techniques* - but unfortunately, they were not careful. Your mind was injured before we could trade you for one of theirs.

We tried everything to reverse the damage but nothing seemed to work, so we hit on the idea of *rebirthing* you, you might say.

We gave you false memories and placed you in a virtual reality clinic for a while. The old John Tyson would know what that is, but I'll explain it anyway.' She searched his face for any sign of understanding then continued.

'We convinced your mind that you were a simple primitive hunter and gave you false memories to back the story up. Then we put you in a chamber where all the sights, sounds, and sensations of your new environment were projected.

'You could not tell the difference between the real and the unreal and we let you lead the life of the hunter while your unconscious mind recovered: or so we hoped.

'We wanted to carefully return you to your normal self. It was the only hope that we had.'

Tyson's brain felt overloaded. His vision blurred and his head ached. 'I ... need to sleep.' He slurred. The first coherent sentence he had used since his return.

Charles woke him at dawn. The weak light barely revealed the stark trees beyond his window.

'Time to get you going.' Charles breezily explained, presenting a glass of yellow liquid as though in compensation. In the other hand he carried a plastic bag with an assortment of clothes. He laid them out one at a time.

'Tell me what they are.'

'Shirt, pants ...' his voice was a croak. He took a sip of the orange juice. 'Singlet, underpants, socks, and shoes.' He managed to conclude.

'There's a jacket too. I'll bring that later. Get yourself dressed and finish your juice. I'll be back in a minute.'

As he dressed, familiarity returned.

Finally, he stood, opened the cupboard door, and regarded himself in the mirror. Yes, this is me he thought wryly, but he still felt the coarse rub of his leather breaches and the weight of his quiver. He rubbed his wrist where once he'd worn a leather band for protection from the bowstring.

Charles and Tyson walked in a garden surrounded by high walls. At first, they said nothing but after a few minutes Charles asked about his life as a hunter. He began to talk, slowly at first but then more quickly, urgently, as though he could recapture something lost. Something he did not want to forget. Something beautiful and precious.

'They tell me it was an illusion' he said, 'but to me it was real. I can still feel the sun and wind and smell my wife's hair ...,' he stopped with a choking sound.

Charles waited patiently until he had collected himself.

'Do you remember anything of your life before you were a hunter?'

'A little, it gets stronger every minute. I think it could come back more quickly, but I don't want to remember the bad parts.'

'Dr. Williams would like you to remember everything as quickly as possible.' said Charles evenly. Tyson listened for a tone of censure but could not detect one.

'The war is not going well, apparently, and they need to know whatever is in your head. I think that the brass are under a lot of pressure. They keep asking Dr. Williams to speed it up ... ' his voice trailed off into silence, then. 'Do you recognise these flowers?'

They were almost back to the entrance when the shots rang out. Tyson did not understand what it was at first, but Charles acted with a speed and agility that surprised the older man. Tyson was flung to the ground behind a garden bench.

An automatic pistol appeared in the big man's hand as though by magic. Another two rapid shots splintered wood from the bench. Charles scanned the overlooking trees and buildings for a target but did not return fire.

'Stay where you are!' he instructed Tyson needlessly, then fingered his lapel microphone and barked instructions.

'Shots fired from the west. Possibly from the white building. Returning client to room. Out.' A crackling acknowledgement was the only response.

After a few seconds they ran for the protection of the entrance. There were no following shots.

Now Tyson was alert. Charles was his only protection he realised. He also knew he'd become the quarry. He must learn fast if he wanted to escape the unknown hunter.

<hr>

'What are you doing?'

'It's called *Pencak Silat*. We used it to warm up before starting the hunt.'

'I don't mean that. You knew martial arts before you were … treated. I mean, why are you exercising, training, instead of resting?'

Tyson made two rapid punches into the empty air; half turned and sent a sudden kick in the same direction. Ali Williams was impressed; anyone in that position would have a very big headache.

'Someone tried to kill me. I have to be ready, and I need a weapon.'

'There is no way I'm going to give you any weapon, Tyson.'

'A Glock 17 like the one Charles uses would be fine.'

'I'm sure it would. It was your favourite in the service too, but you're still not having it. In your mental state you would end up shooting yourself, or someone nearby.'

'In case you haven't noticed. I am much better. My head is clear and I remember most of my former life. Ti-san is someone else, like a brother. Another life … gone.'

'Not quite, it seems; and you're still not getting a weapon.'

Tyson did not pursue the issue. Dropping his arms to his sides he closed his eyes and took three slow and deep breaths.

'John, I need to know what you remember about your assignment. Do you remember anything at all that might be useful?' she sat on the edge of the bed and regarded him with concern.

Tyson shook himself and slumped into a chair opposite, wiping his face on a towel. He was silent for a moment.

'Ali, you told me that the enemy had interfered with my mind. I think you referred to 'subtle techniques?'

'Yes, what about it?'

'Would you say that they know as much about mind ... manipulation as we do?'

'Sure, at least as much, maybe more, they don't have the ethical restraints against experimentation that we do!'

Tyson ignored the superfluous comments and continued.

'Will my mind be permanently damaged?'

'We can't know. We've done everything we can to return you to your earlier condition, but there could always be something hidden deeper. It is a very, very low probability.'

'If they hid something, a suggestion perhaps, that they could trigger later, how would you expect them to protect that? After all, it would be a great asset?'

Williams was thoughtful for a few minutes and then,

'Protect? Well, it would need conditioning in case we uncovered anything, perhaps even a suicide suggestion. But we would detect anything like that. It's impossible.'

'Yes, but if there was something planted would I react violently if exposed. Do you think?'

'Of course! Your life and mission would be at risk. You would probably do anything to prevent that. But it's impossible. Where is all this leading?'

'Oh, I was just wondering.' He rose and poured himself a glass of water from the bottle by the bed.

'We have to find the spy, John. It's the only protection we can give you in the end. Remember what you know, we arrest the spy; you get your life back. Do you remember anything?'

Tyson was looked at her then said quietly,

'No, I didn't remember anything new, Ali.' He paused, 'But I think I know who it is.'

She stood quickly in astonishment,

'What! I don't understand, how, who?'

'It's you, Ali, I'm sorry.'

He was ready when the attack came but still the speed the knife was produced and the ferocity of it almost took him by surprise. With a high-pitched primal screech, her first lunge ripped his pajamas and grazed his chest as he twisted aside. He stepped out of the way and allowed her momentum to carry her past, grabbed her from the rear by her neck and free hand, spun her and pinned her on the bed. It was over in seconds but the knife slashed the mattress uselessly until he pinned that hand as well. Finally, her thrashing legs were also still.

Tyson held her for an eternity; finally, he felt a hand on his shoulder. 'You can let her go now Mr. Tyson. We'll take it from here.'

The room seemed full of people in blue and then it emptied. Tyson sat on the chair and took a deep breath.

'We were watching on the monitor. How did you know she was the spy?'

Tyson looked at him, then chuckled without humour.

'There are no spies, Charles. They engineered my mind to make me into a hunter, how difficult is it to make a spy?'

Charles thought for a minute, 'I've often wondered Mr. Tyson, who is the enemy?'

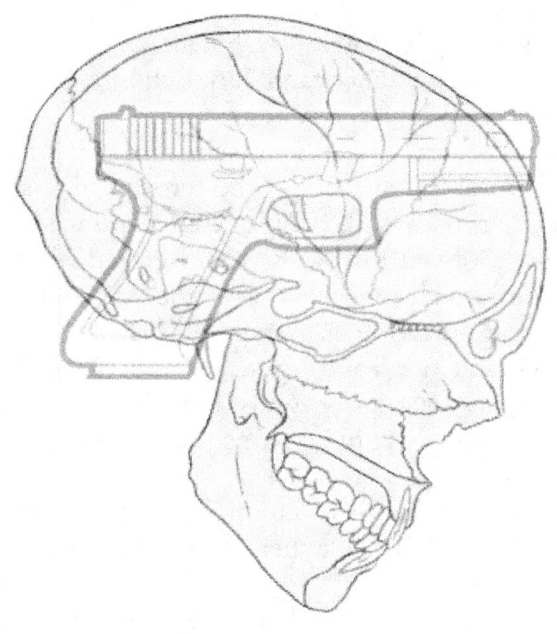

About the Author

Chris Curtis grew up on the North Coast of New South Wales, Australia before he moved to the beautiful harbour city of Sydney and began a technical career. His early life took him to Europe for several years where he developed a life-long interest in travel and languages. He is now gainfully unemployed and writes short fiction stories, teaches English as a foreign language and manages international aid projects.

He lives with his wife in Wollstonecraft, Sydney and his travels often take him to Asia, Europe, and beyond. When he can spare the time, he follows his other interests including fishing and gardening. His published writings have appeared in Amazon eBooks, *Blue Crow* magazine; *Yellow Pearl* anthology; and *The Village Observer* magazine.